The Grah

Ma

with far more triumphs than
hardships.

Shaun

The Graham Family

May your life be filled
with more Triumphs than
hardships.

CPSIA information can be obtained
at www.ICGtesting.com
Printed in the USA
BVOW06s2354070217
475598BV00001B/2/P

9 781682 307861

A Slice of Life

A Short Story Collection

By

Shaun Mehta

authorHOUSE™

1663 LIBERTY DRIVE, SUITE 200
BLOOMINGTON, INDIANA 47403
(800) 839-8640
WWW.AUTHORHOUSE.COM

First published by AuthorHouse 08/10/05

ISBN: 1-4208-3784-2 (sc)

Printed in the United States of America
Bloomington, Indiana

This book is printed on acid-free paper.

Dedication

*To my father and mother.
Your boundless love and
encouragement has helped
me follow my dreams.*

Acknowledgements

I would like to thank Sudhir K. Mehta for his substantive editing.

I am grateful to Jay Chai, Suzanne Medeiros, Joyce Tanjuako, and Alice Young for their assistance in copy editing.

I wish to express my appreciation to Thomas M. Dembie for the design and management of my website: www.shaunmehta.com.

I would also like to thank the following people for their support and encouragement: Kanta Arora; Nalin Bakhle; Joseph Chin; Sue Corke; Dr. Nicole Chitnis; the Dhawan Family; Dr. Michael Fong; Cheryl Fong; the Graham Family; Aimee Fehlner; Susan Jones; the Kalra Family; the Khosla Family; Ralph Kussman; Chris Lynch; Marilena Macchia; the Maingi Family; Jatinder Khanna; Neil Khanna; Kurran Mehta; Richie Mehta; Vishal and Sonal Mehta; Vivek Mehta; Vishwinder and Venu Mehta; Drs. Sudarshan and Bimla Mehta; Ritika Mohan; Nick Patel; Michael Petersen; Mark Pickering; Lisa Pickering; the Sachdev Family; the Sodha Family; Suresh Rajpal; Elaine Rodrigues; Alison Rodrigues; Percy and Maureen Rodrigues; Kiran Sah; Jasmin Sandhu; Dr. Ravi Srivastava; Neeta Tandon; Palma Uhrin; Katie Willis; and my grandmothers, Biji and Nani-Ma.

I wish to give a special thanks to my beloved aunt, Appi Khanna, for her belief in my work.

Author's Note

A Slice of Life addresses such themes as innocence and ignorance, love and perseverance, apathy and cynicism, identity and purpose, courage and fear, and faith and hope.

You may find some shorts thought provoking while others filled with twists. Irrespective of what elements of a short touch you, I hope you will find something in each story that is both intriguing and entertaining.

I have included some non-English words in certain stories for dramatic effect and to enhance the authentic feel of the characters and environment. A glossary is included at the end of the book to clarify these words.

Whether you are curled comfortably in your bed, sitting on the couch in front of the fireplace, or passing time on a train or an airplane, I wish you a most enjoyable read.

Shaun Mehta

Shaun Mehta

Table of Contents

Innocence
&
Ignorance

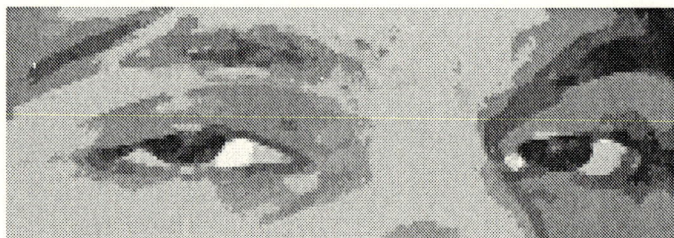

Amal

"Sometimes the poorest of men are the richest."
Anonymous

L ike three generations before him, Amal Arora had
known only one thing—how to be an autorickshaw
wallah. His father had been an autorickshaw driver
from the birth of India's Independence to the
time Prime Minister Indira Gandhi had declared
a State of Emergency. His grandfather had been
an autorickshaw driver during Mahatma Gandhi's
struggle to emancipate India from British rule. Even
Amal's great-grandfather had been a rickshaw driver
during the height of the British Raj, although during
his tenure it took one's legs rather than engines to
power a rickshaw.

Although the political landscape of the subcontinent altered dramatically with each generation, the
purpose of the Arora men had not.

Throughout his childhood, Amal's father had
shown him that it was an autorickshaw wallah's duty
to transport people through the capital of India as
safely and quickly as possible. It was critical to reach
the destination with a satisfied customer, even if it
meant losing money.

Whether it was driving students to school, shoppers
to the market, worshippers to their place of worship,
or employees to work, Amal learned from his father to
understand and embrace the small yet vital role that,
he believed, God had assigned him.

Crippled with arthritis near the end of his life,
Amal's father had explained to his son that an Arora
existed for three fundamental reasons: to perform his
job as an autorickshaw wallah to the best of his ability,

to save for his daughter's dowry until she was ready for marriage, and to continue to keep the belly of his family full.

Even a decade after his father's cremation, Amal lived by these three simple objectives. He had no other ambitions or wishes.

"Amal, why don't you ever go home and sleep with your wife?" Raju asked.

Amal and Raju had parked their autorickshaws in front of India Gate.

The monument bore the names of eighty-two thousand Indian soldiers that had perished during World War I and other military campaigns at the beginning of the twentieth century. Located in the verdant heart of New Delhi, India Gate was a popular spot for locals and tourists.

"Well? Don't avoid my question, yaar."

Raju inhaled his bidi with relish as he waited for a response.

"What?" Amal yawned.

He removed *The Times of India* that had covered his face as he snoozed.

"Why don't you ever go home and sleep with your wife?"

"Areé, what rubbish! I went only two days ago, bhai," Amal reminded his childhood friend.

He emerged from his autorickshaw and stretched his sore back and neck.

"Yes, because it was Sunday. You only spend one night a week at home. Why?"

"Areé, bhai, come now! You know Sunday tends to be the slowest day in the city. I would lose too much time driving to and from home every day, hain-nah?"

Amal and his family lived in a teeming slum on the outskirts of Old Delhi.

"But don't you yearn for the warmth of your wife at night, rather than being crumpled up in your autorickshaw?" Raju asked.

He slowly exhaled to maximize the effect of the brown-leafed tobacco.

Amal contemplated an appropriate response. He loved the three-wheeler he had inherited from his father nearly as much as his wife and children, although he would never admit it.

"Well? Don't try to avoid my question, Amal."

Amal sighed, weary of his friend's probing questions.

"Bhai, the extra hundred rupees I earn each day are more comforting than any pillow or blanket...or even my wife's bosom," he said with a mischievous grin.

Raju smiled and flicked the remnants of his bidi. He motioned Amal to hand over *The Times of India* and sat down in his autorickshaw to read the newspaper.

Dozens of children splashed in a pool beside India Gate to escape the relentless summer heat, despite dusk settling over the capital. Amal wiped the sweat from his brow as he watched the children play.

Amal suddenly remembered that the fuel tank of his autorickshaw was nearly empty. He lifted the black cushioned passenger seat in the back of his three-wheeler and extracted a water bottle full of fuel from beneath it.

He scowled as he thought of how most drivers filled their tanks at petrol stations while they had passengers in their autorickshaws. This allowed them to charge more rupees. Not only was it dishonest, but it also wasted the precious time of the disgruntled passengers and ultimately harmed the reputation of *all* autorickshaw wallahs. Amal had once proposed at a union meeting to abolish the practice and was stunned by the hostile opposition he had received.

As Amal filled the fuel tank, he continued to watch with amusement as the children played in the water nearby.

The magnificent silhouette of the forty-two meter stone arch, set in front of the blazing orange-purple hued sky, filled Amal's heart with peace. India Gate was one of his favorite locations in New Delhi.

"Areé, auto wallah!"

Amal looked up.

A bald, decrepit hunched man in a ragged dhoti limped slowly towards him. He used a crooked cane for support.

Amal replaced the empty bottle underneath the seat and reached out to assist the man into the back of the autorickshaw.

"Sit down, sit down!" the old man said. "I'm not that crippled that I need your help."

"Yes, sahib."

Amal returned to the driver's seat.

"Take me to Connaught Place," the old man said sternly.

"Yes, sahib."

The autorickshaw wallah triggered the meter and pulled the black lever beside him to start the three-wheeler. The small engine buzzed to life.

Amal closed his eyes for a moment to savor the sound of the motor. He had spent years modifying the engine to enhance its performance and minimize fuel consumption.

"What are you doing? Meditating? Move!" the old man barked.

"Yes, sahib."

Amal waved to Raju as he pulled the rickshaw into traffic.

"Beautiful evening, isn't it, sahib?"

"I'm not paying you for conversation, understand?" snapped the old man.

"Yes, sahib. My apologies."

Amal extended his left arm out of the autorickshaw to signal he was making a left turn off the roundabout that surrounded India Gate. He turned onto Kasturba Gandhi Marg, a wide tree-lined boulevard.

As they passed Canning Road traffic grinded to a halt.

Amal braked to a stop.

The engine automatically shut off to conserve fuel.

The old man broke into a wheezing, hacking cough.

"Damn these fumes!" he gasped.

"Sahib, here...take this," Amal said.

He handed the old man a clean white handkerchief that he kept for his passengers.

"This will help you breathe."

"Areé, why have we stopped? What's the problem?" the old man demanded, his voice muffled from the handkerchief that covered his mouth.

Amal leaned out and looked past the honking cars, black smoke spewing lorries, ringing bicycles, overcrowded scooters, yelping dogs, mooing cows, cursing pedestrians, and other autorickshaws. He grimaced at the grisly sight that had created the jammed mass of steel and flesh.

"A truck struck an elephant, sahib," Amal said. "It has blocked the road."

"Well, get me out of here. I don't care how. Do it now."

"Yes, sahib."

Amal knew every inch of his vehicle and used his skill to slowly move the three-wheeler through spaces between traffic that the old man didn't think existed. With savvy, Amal maneuvered the autorickshaw through the clogged street, and turned onto Firoz Shah Road, which was far less congested.

"Drive faster," the old man ordered.

Amal quietly obeyed, but was careful not to accelerate past the speed limit.

Ten minutes later, Amal turned from Janpath Road onto the outer ring road of Connaught Place known as Connaught Circus.

Swelling with people, Connaught Place was the business and tourist center of New Delhi. It consisted of two major roundabouts that dissected a uniform series of ancient colonnaded buildings filled with shops, banks, restaurants, and commercial offices.

Amal patiently slowed down and smiled as he absorbed the cacophony of activity that made Connaught Place so vibrant.

"All phony, lying, money-sucking leaches," the old man muttered, snapping Amal from the trance of the surrounding sights and sounds.

"Forgive the intrusion, sahib, but where exactly in Connaught Place would you like me to drop you?" Amal asked as they circled Connaught Circus for a third time.

"Huh? Stupid fool, you missed the turn to Nehru Park!"

"Sahib?"

"I told you I wanted to go to Nehru Park in the center of Connaught Place."

"Are you sure, sahib? I do not remember that request."

"How dare you call me a liar!"

"No, sahib. I am not calling you that at all. It is my mistake. I apologize."

"What is your rickshaw number? I'll report you for your incompetence and this outrage."

"The number is written on the metal divider in front of you, sahib," Amal replied calmly.

The old man pulled out a dull, stubby pencil and a dirty notepad from his frayed shirt. He squinted as he read the numbers and scribbled onto the paper.

"All autorickshaw wallahs are cheating, incompetent scoundrels," he mumbled with irritation.

Amal made a right turn and drove past the inner circle road to the center of Connaught Place.

Staying quiet as the old man continued to rant, Amal pulled the autorickshaw to the curb in front of Nehru Park.

"Nehru Park, Connaught Place, sahib."

"How much?" the old man demanded once he had disembarked.

Amal studied the meter in the waning light. "Forty-seven rupees, sahib."

"For your incompetence I will only pay you thirty-seven rupees. And I'm going to keep your handkerchief as well. What do you think of that, eh?" he asked, as he poked Amal with his cane.

"As I was mistaken about the destination, you may pay me anything that satisfies you, sahib."

The old man stared at Amal as if he was crazy.

"What kind of autorickshaw wallah are you?"

"One that believes that not *all* autorickshaw drivers are cheating, incompetent scoundrels, sahib."

The old man snorted with disbelief.

"You're a naïve fool who'll die impoverished," he said.

He rummaged through his pockets until he found several tattered bills. He studied the money in the semi-darkness and handed the bills to Amal.

"This should cover it."

"Sahib, wait, you gave me fifty rupees," Amal said.

"Huh, what? What did you say?"

"Here is your change, sahib. And I have three rupees for you as well."

The old man raised his eyebrow with disbelief. For the first time, he properly studied the bearded, dark-skinned man wearing a stained white undershirt and a simple dhoti.

"Keep the three rupees."

"Sahib, I can not," Amal said.

He pulled out three one-rupee coins from a tin can he kept hidden in front of his autorickshaw.

"Here, please take this. You were dissatisfied with my service."

"Never mind that. I told you to keep the change!"

"I can not," Amal said. "You felt the ride was worth thirty-seven rupees and my handkerchief, and that is how much I will be paid."

The old man pocketed the money.

"What's your name?"

"Amal, sahib. Amal Arora."

"Amal, eh? An uncommon and strange name. Was your mother drunk when she named you?"

"My mother died during my birth, sahib. I was named and raised by my father."

The old man stared at the autorickshaw wallah with a piercing glare.

"Have a good evening, sahib," Amal said.

"Hmph!" the cantankerous man snorted.

He turned and furiously tapped his cane against the pavement as he limped into Nehru Park.

*   *   *   *   *

Whistling to the song from the latest Bollywood hit playing from his tape deck, Amal noticed an impeccably dressed middle-aged man signaling for an autorickshaw.

Amal ejected the tape as he pulled to the curb.

His smiling eyes warmly glanced through the rear-view mirror at the passenger getting into the back of the autorickshaw.

"Good afternoon, sahib," Amal said.

"Do you understand English?"

"Yes, sahib."

"Excellent. Take me to the Taj Mahal Hotel."

"Sahib?" Amal said, certain he had misheard.

The middle-aged man leaned forward and said: "I'm Mr. Agrawal, personal attorney of Mr. G.K. Jayaram."

"I am happy to hear that, sahib, but—"

"Please, call me Mr. Agrawal."

Amal frowned, beginning to feel uncomfortable.

"Where would you like me to take you?"

"I told you, the Taj Hotel."

"I do not understand, sahib. We are parked in front of the Taj Hotel."

"Your name is Amal Arora, correct?"

"Yes, sahib. How did you know this?" Amal asked anxiously.

"Come inside the hotel. I have offices in there. We can speak more comfortably and in private. I'll explain everything."

"Sahib, that is not possible. I have to make an earning for my family. It is noon, a very busy time."

"I understand, Amal, but this is most important. I must insist."

"You have still not answered my question. How do you know who I am? I have paid my fee to the Godfather on time this month. There must be some misunderstanding. Please, tell him this."

Mr. Agrawal laughed.

"No, Amal, don't be alarmed. This has nothing to do with the Godfather. Now, listen to me. Do you know G.K. Jayaram?"

"No, sahib, I do not."

"You drove him once, about a year ago. He was a very old man."

"Driven countless old men throughout Delhi, sahib."

"Yes, but this old man was very eccentric and ill-tempered. I believe he took this from you," Mr. Agrawal said.

He removed a white handkerchief from his briefcase.

Amal's eyes widened.

"Oh yes, I remember him now. He was in a most disagreeable mood that evening, upset at my poor service."

Amal paused and frowned.

"I still do not understand what all of this has to do with me. I am a very simple man, sahib."

"I know, Amal. Listen, I've spent much time searching for you. I must speak to you in private."

"How did you find me, sahib? There are thousands of rickshaw wallahs in Delhi."

"Mr. Jayaram wrote down your rickshaw number to file a complaint in his notepad. It took some time for us to discover this. And then it took more time to find you and learn your routine. Normally you always come by the Taj Hotel around this time of day. Amazing that you were always underneath my nose and it still took me so much time to find you."

Mr. Agrawal adjusted his spectacles and smiled.

"So, you will come with me, yes? I promise it will not take long, Amal."

Amal took several moments to consider his decision. Mr. Agrawal was pleasant and seemed to be speaking the truth. But one thing still bothered him.

"I would grant your request, sahib, but I can't leave my autorickshaw unattended. It is my livelihood."

"Don't concern yourself, Amal. It'll be safe here. There're security guards everywhere."

Mr. Agrawal stepped out of the autorickshaw.

Amal looked around, distraught. He did not know what to do. The thought of leaving his prized possession with a stranger was distressing. Unless home on a Sunday, he had never left his autorickshaw unattended in the decade he had operated it.

"Amal?"

"One moment, please, sahib," Amal pleaded.

He wondered how to escape his predicament.

Amal noticed his friend Raju parking his autorickshaw across the street in front of the samosa kiosk, a popular hangout for many rickshaw wallahs to have a snack, smoke, or gossip.

"I will leave the autorickshaw with my friend, sahib. Please wait one moment."

Before Mr. Agrawal could respond, Amal turned on the three-wheeler. He did a U-turn and parked his autorickshaw beside his friend.

"Amal," Raju called out as he lit a bidi. "Do you want something to eat?"

"Bhai, can you watch my rickshaw? It is most important."

"Areé, too much! No need to ask, nah? You know I

will take good care of it."

"Thank you, bhai. I will be back soon."

Amal crossed the bustling street to join Mr. Agrawal. As they walked towards the hotel's entrance, a little girl in rags leaped in front of them. She held a naked, screaming baby in her arms.

"Oh my!" Mr. Agrawal exclaimed.

"Please, sahib. Alms for the needy?" the girl desperately asked in Hindi. "We are hungry. Please, sahib."

"Get out of here!" growled the Taj Hotel's Sikh doorman. He stepped menacingly towards the girl.

The small girl cried out with fear. Fiercely clutching the baby, she bolted down the street.

"Apologies for the intrusion, Mr. Agrawal," rumbled the towering Sikh in English as he straightened his red cummerbund and turban. "Those tiny beggars are relentless scavengers."

"Quite alright. Thank you," Mr. Agrawal said gratefully.

Avoiding eye contact with the intimidating Sikh who opened the door for them, Amal walked into the opulent Taj Hotel.

*   *   *   *   *

Mr. Agrawal gestured Amal towards the leather chair in front of his expansive desk.

"Please, have a seat."

Amal sat down and shifted uncomfortably. He wistfully thought about the simple cushion on his autorickshaw. He hoped Raju was watching his three-wheeler carefully and yearned to escape these lavish surroundings.

"Amal, I regret to inform you that G.K. Jayaram passed away from a massive heart-attack a month ago."

"I am saddened by this news, sahib. But, what does this have to do with me?"

"Everything will be explained by this letter that Mr. Jayaram wrote specifically addressed to you."

Mr. Agrawal extracted the folded letter from his briefcase and handed it to Amal.

"He had very direct instructions in his Will that you were to read this before I answered any of your questions."

Amal slowly unfolded the paper, and stared at the writing:

Dear Amal,

I don't expect you to remember me, but I certainly remember that day you drove me to Connaught Place.

Amal, I dedicated my entire life to acquiring billions of rupees and a vast empire in the hope of improving my India. And as I grew in wealth and power, I never hesitated in making the necessary decision. But now, as I come to the end of my life, I have a most difficult decision to make.

Your father named you very wisely, Amal. As I am sure you know, your name means many things, such as: 'bright,' 'clean,' and 'pure.' Your name also means 'hope,' 'wish,' and 'dream.'

Amal, I have 6 children, 14 grandchildren, and I employ 38,000 employees—all deceitful, greedy leeches. None of these people possess the 'pure,' 'clean,' and 'bright' soul that you have. Amal, you have fulfilled my 'wish' and 'dream' to find 'hope' in this world. I've spent years searching the streets of New Delhi to find someone like you. Despite your precarious financial situation—yes, I had an investigator look into your affairs—you possess an honesty and peace that my crores of rupees couldn't buy. Not many people would admit that their customer had 'accidentally' given them additional money, especially after I treated you with such insensitivity. And none would refuse to accept a meager tip after committing such a kind act.

But you did. Amal, I know hundreds of wealthy people that would spill blood for money, and despite being in dire need to provide for your family, your morals prevailed. I am deeply touched.

You're a rare commodity, Amal. Despite having so little, you clearly are filled with happiness and tranquility, as if you're living your dream. You showed me that there's still hope for humanity, and for this gift, I am eternally grateful. But I'm not merely a man of compliments, Amal. I'm a man who shows his gratitude by action.

I, Ganesh Kumar Jayaram, of sound mind and body bequeath 100 crore rupees to Amal Arora out of my Estate.

Amal, don't squander and waste this opportunity as I did. Use this wealth with the same wisdom your father used when he named and raised you into the exemplary man I had the privilege to meet.

Mr. Agrawal is a competent attorney, and he has drafted a Will that can not be contested by even the shrewdest of my children. However, if you don't wish to have Mr. Agrawal represent you or your Estate, please feel free to find any other legal representative you desire.

God bless you and your wise father.

Gratefully yours.

Sri Ganesh Kumar Jayaram.

July 8th, New Delhi

The lawyer silently observed Amal. He wondered how the autorickshaw wallah would react to the discovery that he had become one of the wealthiest men in the subcontinent.

Amal looked up from the letter and stared blankly at the lawyer.

"Are you okay, Amal?" Mr. Agrawal asked.

"Yes, thank you, sahib."

"Do you have any questions?"

"No, sahib."

Amal put his palms together and stood up.

"Namasté."

"N-Namasté?" Mr. Agrawal echoed, startled. "No, wait."

"I must go, sahib."

"Please don't forget to contact me if you have any questions. We've provided excellent legal services for Mr. Jayaram and his businesses for over thirty years. Contact me to discuss how you want the estate dealt with!" the lawyer cried as Amal walked out of his luxurious office.

The lawyer slammed his hand against the desk with frustration.

"Shit!"

The partners are going to crucify me for losing that account, he thought.

Mr. Agrawal sighed and scratched his head.

He envied Amal and wondered what the rickshaw wallah would do with the fortune.

*   *   *   *   *

Amal walked quickly out of the hotel, anxious to return to his autorickshaw.

He smiled as he saw the black-and-yellow vehicle glimmering in the sun, parked where he had left it.

I must wash it before I sleep tonight, he thought. *It's far too dusty.*

As Amal crossed the street, the little beggar girl holding the wailing baby ran up to him.

"Please, sahib. We are very hungry," she begged.

His eyes fixed on his autorickshaw, Amal pulled out a ten rupee bill and handed it to the grateful beggar.

The little girl noticed the folded letter clutched in Amal's hand.

"We were given a pen by a foreigner earlier today, sahib. But we have no paper to draw."

Without hesitation, Amal handed her the folded letter.

"Oh thank you, sahib. God bless you," the girl said happily.

She stopped and admired the fine quality of the paper. Her eyes danced as she imagined the hours of fun she would have doodling. Even the baby in her arms stopped crying, curious at his sister's acquisition.

Amal climbed into his autorickshaw and took a deep breath.

He thanked Raju and pulled the lever to turn on the three-wheeler.

Amal revved the engine of his beloved vehicle and pulled into the traffic. He was unaware of the beggar girl chasing after him.

Raju lowered his newspaper as the beggar holding the sniffling baby dejectedly walked past him.

"What's the matter, girl? Why were you chasing Amal's autorickshaw?"

"Sahib, this paper that kind rickshaw wallah gave me has writing on it. Is it something important? Do you think he gave it to me by mistake?"

"I doubt it," Raju laughed and turned back to his newspaper. "Amal can't read."

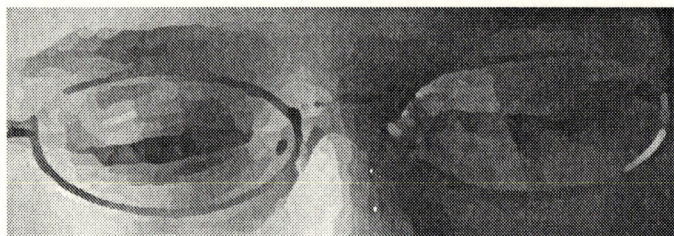

Inseparable

"Sibling relationships...outlast marriages, survive the death of parents, resurface after quarrels that would sink any friendship. They flourish in a thousand incarnations of closeness and distance, warmth, loyalty and distrust."
Erica E. Goode

Kris Kumar awoke in a panic. He furiously squinted until the blurry display of the glowing digital numbers came into focus.

6:24 a.m.

A gasp of delight escaped his lips. He clamped his hand over his mouth, afraid that he had made too much noise.

He listened for sound, but heard nothing. The house was silent. The frosted bedroom window was dark. Unlike the past several pre-dawn winter mornings, there was no bone chilling, howling wind. It was as if the world was a vacuum, devoid of sound.

Kris threw off his Harry Potter blanket, put on his glasses, and waited for his eyes to adjust to the darkness.

Move, Kris, move, he urged himself. *Time is short.*

He got out of bed too quickly and winced as his mattress creaked with protest.

He froze, his bare-feet cold against the wooden floor. He listened for any small movement or disturbance.

Silence.

Kris grabbed his towel and turned the doorknob of his bedroom door. The rusting hinges had caused several heartbreaking losses in the past. To avoid making the same critical mistake, Kris had oiled the hinges the previous night.

The door opened with fluid silence. Although pleased by his own cunning, he resisted smiling. He was afraid he would jinx his advantage.

Craning his neck, Kris looked down the hallway at the coveted bathroom. The door was open, the entrance a black rectangle.

Kris crept towards the bathroom, tiptoeing with painstaking care to ensure none of the floorboards betrayed his presence.

As he approached a closed bedroom door on his right, Kris glanced at the portrait of his parents hanging outside the bathroom wall; their benevolent smiles filled with pride for his imminent victory.

This time, Kris could not resist returning their smile. The euphoria of triumph never felt so delicious.

Kris yelped with surprise and pain as he stepped on a piece of Lego. Like a field of landmines, hundreds of pieces had been scattered on the floor.

He instinctively reached for his throbbing foot when the unmistakable sound of little feet pounding against the wooden floor came from the nearby bedroom.

Kris broke into an awkward run-limp as his little brother, Anu, burst from his bedroom and crashed into him.

Anu's five inch shorter body smashed into his brother with full force.

Nearly knocked off his feet, Kris hit the staircase banister.

Anu moved past him.

Kris flailed at his little brother's kurta pajama. The

fabric brushed against his outstretched fingers and escaped his reach.

"Noooo!" Kris cried as Anu slammed the bathroom door shut.

Kris lunged for the door in one desperate attempt to push his way into the bathroom. The dreadful sound of the engaged lock destroyed any sliver of hope.

Defeated, Kris slumped to the ground and rubbed the bottom of his aching foot.

Through the door, Anu's sweet, high-pitched voice was seized with a fit of giggles.

"I win again, bhai!"

Kris stared incredulously at the bathroom door, amazed that he had been foiled by his brother's ingenious trap.

He stood up, laughing, an amiable loser.

"Yeah, you did, chottu," he said affectionately, using the Hindi word for 'small one'. "But, I'll get you tomorrow."

"No, you won't!" Anu gasped between his laughter. "You have to make my breakfast and lunch again!"

"Yeah, yeah, I'm going," Kris muttered with feigned irritation.

He was astonished that a seven-year old had foiled him again.

"Can I have butter *and* honey on my toast, bhai?" asked the muffled voice over the sound of running water. "And no mustard on my sandwich, *please!*"

"What was that, chottu? *No* honey and *lots* of mustard? Okay, you got it!" Kris said as he descended the stairs towards the kitchen.

"Ha, ha, very funny, bhai. Hello? Bhai? *Bhai!*"

*   *   *   *   *

"Hey, *yeahr*, are you sure I can stay over?" Jeremiah Zimmerman shouted over the ruckus of activity within the rumbling school bus. Concern filled his chubby face.

Kris turned and placed his knees on the green soft plastic so he could look over the top of the seat and face his friend sitting behind him. He pushed his eyeglasses back up the bridge of his nose.

"Jere, man, if you're going to watch Hindi movies, then learn to speak properly, eh? It's 'yaar' not 'yeahr'!"

Two sparkling black eyes below an oversized blue toque popped up from behind the back of the bus seat to face Kris's friend.

"Yeah, Jere!" Anu exclaimed, shaking his head with disapproval.

"Oh, okay..." Jeremiah said.

He paused and looked thoughtfully at the rushing snowy, suburban landscape.

"...Um, Kris, what does 'yaar' mean, anyways?"

Anu rolled his eyes and disappeared behind the seat.

"It means 'friend,' yaar," Kris said. "And don't worry. My parents are really cool about things like this."

"You asked them?" Jeremiah said.

"Well, no. We only see them on the weekends so I didn't get a chance."

"What do you mean you only see them on the weekends, Kris? Where are they?"

"They own a convenient store, and work every day very late. When they come home, Anu and I are sleeping. And when we get ready for school, they're still asleep."

"But *who* feeds you?" Jeremiah asked, aghast.

"Our grandmother cooks us dinner," Kris said, wondering why Jeremiah looked so upset. "And *she* said it was okay that you slept over. She's expecting you."

"She makes the best chapatti and yellow daal!" Anu said.

He smacked his lips nosily.

"That's because that's *all* you ever want to eat for dinner!" Kris complained. "Why don't you try something else? Do it for your big bhai, okay?"

"Yellow daal, yellow daal, yellow daal!"

Kris sighed and turned back to his Jewish friend.

"So you're coming over, right?"

"And what about your afternoon snack? Or, breakfast and lunch? Who makes *that*?"

Anu beamed and Kris scowled.

That morning, Kris awoke to Anu shaking him awake. He was stunned to find his little brother dressed and his hair slicked smartly from a recent shower. Kris could not understand how he had slept in until he realized his clock had been set an hour behind—a covert operation Anu must have successfully executed late last night as he was dreaming of saving the magically inept Harry Potter from the evil clutches of Lord Voldemort.

"Tomorrow's Saturday, and my mother will make the best omelet for us, okay?" Kris said.

Jeremiah still looked skeptical.

"Come on, Jere! Look, with my parents not home we can do *anything*. My grandmother gives us *a lot* of freedom. I'll even set up the tent in the bedroom to sleep in."

Jeremiah's eyes grew wide as he imagined all the adventures they could have with the tent.

"Really?" he said.

"Yeah, don't worry, yaar!" Kris enthused.

"Don't worry, yaar!" Anu mimicked.

"Okay," Jeremiah said as he stared solemnly at his rumbling potbelly. "But there better be *good* food to eat."

"Yellow daal, yellow daal, yellow daal!"

As the school bus made a wide turn into a picturesque residential neighborhood, Kris fell back into his seat and fretted over Anu's winter clothes.

Despite being only nine-years old, Kris took his role as the older brother seriously.

"Hey, stop fiddling so much, chottu," he ordered, as he pulled Anu's zipper to the top of the puffy jacket.

Flooded in afternoon sunlight, Anu was sweating.

"I'm hot!" he complained.

"Do you want to *freeze* and catch a cold when you go outside?" Kris asked.

He tightly covered his younger brother's mouth and neck with a woolen scarf with such effectiveness that only Anu's eyes were visible.

The bus stopped in front of a quaint house with a piercing screech.

The three boys disembarked.

"Now, chottu, don't forget to—"

"I know."

Anu's black eyes glared at his older brother before taking his hand to cross the street.

"Hey, what's 'yellow daal', anyways?" Jeremiah asked apprehensively while he chased after his friends. "Is it kosher?"

*   *   *   *   *

The large tent, which dominated the darkened bedroom, glowed red. Dancing shadows flashed across the translucent crimson fabric.

"The Blair Witch is going to get you!" Jere cried, turning on his flashlight.

His contorted face materialized from the darkness.

"Make him stop, bhai!" Anu whimpered, hiding within his sleeping bag.

"Stop scaring my brother, Jere," Kris intoned mechanically from the opposite side of the tent, absorbed in his novel.

A flashlight tucked underneath Kris's chin enabled him to precariously balance the immense *Harry Potter and the Goblet of Fire* that he had received for his birthday.

"I'm just having fun, Kris," Jere scowled. "There's nothing to be afraid of. We're *inside* a house in a city, not in the middle of a forest in Maryland! Besides, he likes it—*he's* the one who keeps bugging me to scare him."

"He's *only* seven, Jere," Kris said, his attention still on the book. "*Everything* scares him."

"It does not!" replied a muffled, insulted voice from within the sleeping bag. "I *like* being scared."

"Then just look at Jere," Kris said, as he turned the page. "There's nothing scarier."

Like a jack-in-the-box, Anu's head popped out of the sleeping bag shaking in a fit of adorable laughter.

Kris's heart swelled with joy. His little brother's laugh was like music for his soul and very contagious.

Despite the remark being at Jeremiah's expense, he also laughed.

"Oh, I'm scary looking, am I?" he said with a sly grin, tackling Kris.

Soon all three boys were playfully wrestling and laughing, entangled in each other's legs and arms.

A door slammed fiercely from somewhere downstairs, and the three boys fell silent. Their flailing limbs and twisted bodies froze. As angry voices suddenly reverberated through the house, the boys scrambled into their sleeping bags and turned off the flashlights.

"What's going on?" Jeremiah asked, his eyes wide.

"Our parents are home," Kris said.

"They're fighting again," Anu whispered.

The argument gained intensity, breaking into furious shouting. It finally ended with dishes shattering against some hard surface.

The front door suddenly slammed with such fury that the entire house shuddered.

The sound of footsteps ascended the staircase.

The three boys squeezed their eyes shut pretending to be asleep. Kris yearned to shut his ears from the sound of his mother weeping as she walked past his bedroom and quietly closed the door to the master bedroom.

Far more unsettling than the yelling was the dreadful silence that encompassed the frightened boys. The boys exhaled a collective sigh of relief as Kris turned on his flashlight.

Jeremiah gawked at Kris and Anu, open-mouthed, his eyes nearly popping out of his head.

"What, Jere? What is it?" Kris said, wishing his friend would stop staring at him that way.

"Are your parents going to get a divorce?" Jeremiah asked.

Kris laughed uneasily.

"What? Of course not! They always disagree. It's normal."

"They're 'inseppable!'" Anu added, nodding vigorously with agreement.

Jeremiah gave Anu a quizzical look.

"Huh?"

"In...sep...ar...a...ble," Anu pronounced carefully as he watched his older brother mouth out the word.

"Inseparable!" he repeated, grinning. "Like us!"

Kris smiled broadly, his chest bubbling with love and pride for his brother.

"They don't sound inseparable to me," Jeremiah said, frowning.

Anu's smile vanished.

"Listen, Jere, they had an arranged marriage," Kris said.

"Uh huh."

"In *India!*"

"So?"

Kris sighed.

"For someone who watches Bollywood movies all the time, you don't learn much, do you?"

"Hey, what does that mean?" Jere demanded.

"There are *no* divorces among Indian marriages," Kris explained. "It's unheard of. Do you know any Indian parents that are divorced? They're inseparable until death."

"Death," Anu repeated.

"But they sounded *really* angry," Jeremiah persisted. "My mother said that when a mother and father stop loving each other, they get divorced."

"They disagree on lots of things, but they *still* love each other," Kris said. "See, with arranged marriages divorces are...are *forbidden*. It's like a...a law by God."

"God," Anu said, nodding solemnly.

Jeremiah snorted with disbelief, unconvinced.

Kris was exasperated. Why was Jere being so difficult? He decided to try another approach.

"Look, Jere, in India—"

"Kris, this is not India!"

Kris glared at his friend. From the corner of his vision he noticed the dejected look on his brother's face. His irritation dissolved.

"Hey, Jere, forget it, okay? Let's not do this."

Jeremiah guiltily eyed Anu and nodded.

"Yeah, sorry. I didn't mean it...*yeahr*," he said with an exaggerated Indian accent.

A hint of a giggle escaped Anu.

"Now, do you *really* want to get scared, chottu?" Kris asked in a chilling, deep voice that he had perfected last Halloween. Anu adored this.

Anu's face brightened. He scrambled into his sleeping bag until only half of his face was visible.

Kris switched off the flashlight.

Jeremiah gasped and Anu squealed with fearful delight as blackness enveloped them.

"I have a story that will make the Blair Witch seem like Mrs. Santa Clause," Kris growled menacingly as he smiled in the darkness.

*   *   *   *   *

The vibrations of the silent alarm underneath his pillow startled Kris awake.

He fell out of bed and stood in one motion.

The light of dawn bathed his room. Birds chirped brightly at the promise of another gorgeous spring day.

He grabbed his glasses with one hand and his towel with the other.

Kris had learned through the preparation of countless breakfasts and lunches that he could not outwit or outsmart Anu's calculating mind. Speed and strength were his weapons.

Kris ran through his bedroom door, which he now kept open. Who needed to oil hinges when one didn't even need to open the door!

He noticed that the bathroom doorway was unlit, still waiting for that morning's champion.

Lips pressed firmly with determination, Kris broke into a dash.

As he passed his brother's open bedroom door, he skidded to a stop.

Stunned, Kris stared at the empty bedroom. It was devoid of all furniture or presence that Anu had ever resided there.

He had forgotten. How could he have forgotten?

He turned to his parent's portrait.

The photograph had been roughly torn in half. His smiling father now stood by himself.

A feeling of empty hollowness swelled painfully within his chest, as if a piece of his heart was missing.

Kris noticed a bright object lying against the wall.

With a sad smile, he stepped on the piece of Lego.

He closed his eyes and relished the feeling of the hard plastic stabbing his flesh. He tried to recreate the fond memories of so many prior mornings.

They were inseparable, he reminded himself. That's what he had told his brother countless times. Nothing could tear them apart.

Then why did he feel so empty, void, as if a black hole was sucking his warm memories and feelings relentlessly?

I'm sorry, Anu. You trusted me and I failed you.

Kris opened his glistening eyes.

The bathroom door closed.

The lock engaged.

Love
&
Perseverance

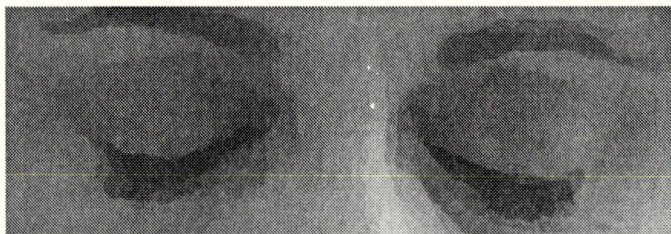

Anniversary

*"Rejoice with your family in the
beautiful land of life."*

Albert Einstein

The display on the bedside clock clicks to 6:45 a.m., triggering the alarm.

Sitting at the small cherry-wood desk in my bedroom, I ignore the incessant beeping.

I sign my name on the bottom of the thick paper, and slide it into the envelope bearing my mother's name. I delicately place the envelope on the dresser.

I stretch and yawn before walking around the neatly made bed to turn off the alarm. As I tightly wrap my robe over my nightdress, I glance at the letter across the room.

Filled with anticipation throughout the night, I had not been able to sleep. After much deliberation, I had spent the pre-dawn writing the letter, oblivious to the waning moon, chirping birds, and growing activity on the street below that marked the end of the night. Writing my thoughts on paper had calmed me.

I smile as the sunlight streaming through the drapes warms my face.

It is the start of a new day—*the* day.

Feeling euphoric, I walk with a light step into the bathroom to begin my morning ritual.

After using the loo, I scrub my hands with soap under the tap for three minutes. Vigorous hand washing is a custom I have instilled in my sons—Harry, 12, and Daniel, 10—since the moment they learned to walk.

'Harry! Daniel! Come here and wash your hands. Scrub them hard until they're pink. Cleanliness is a virtue,' I would remind them.

'*Daaaaad!*' they would protest, searching for their father's support.

'*Listen to your mother, boys,*' David, my husband, would say cheerfully without looking up from his newspaper.

'*Move it you two, I mean it,*' I would admonish. '*And don't forget to wash that grime off your faces. We're not paupers, are we?*'

'*Aw, Mum!*' they would whine in unison.

I grin at the image of their sweet, round faces scowling at me before they obediently march to the bathroom, grumbling and muttering under their breaths.

I apply facial cream, and frown at the shiny, pasty reflection in the mirror.

Have I been too harsh, too regimental in upbringing the boys?

Between the two of us, David always was the good one, slyly sparing the boys from punishments I sentenced them to. It drove me crazy, but I was secretly thankful that he provided a welcome balance to my authoritarian parenting. We instinctively understood that he was the fun, light-hearted one, and I was the disciplinarian. United, we provided a balanced and nurturing environment for our sons to flourish and prosper.

I dismiss such thoughts from my mind.

Now is not the time, I remind myself. *There's much to do.*

As I brush my teeth, I mentally list the things that need to be done on this momentous day. I decide to begin by watering the plants and preparing breakfast.

I walk into the yellow-tiled kitchen, my favourite room in the cozy house. When David and I bought the house, we had gutted the dismally bleak kitchen, and spent thousands of pounds renovating it. We had even torn down the back wall and added a splendid solarium.

The kitchen and solarium is ablaze with illumination, and the three-dozen plants thrive in the nurturing light.

I water each plant lovingly, and wave cheerfully through the back window at my neighbor, Mrs. Wildes, who curiously peaks her pruned face over the fence. Although she is a nosy, gossipy old woman, I often invite her for tea and enjoy her adventurous—and often exaggerated—tales as a volunteer nurse in France during World War II.

I put the empty watering jug aside and decide to turn on the small tele on the kitchen counter. I am tired of listening to silence.

"This is the BBC news, for Friday, June 23rd, 2003. Good morning," broadly smiles the handsome anchor, his perfect, bleached teeth a little too white. "Our top story: In Northern Ireland, the Ulster Freedom Fighters suspends its threat to call off the ceasefire. The statement followed an appeal from the Ulster Democratic Party, which has links to the UFF, not to break its truce..."

The news on the tele fades into the background as I slice a fresh grapefruit in half. I sprinkle brown sugar on top of the slices and place it in the center of the kitchen table.

Just the way David likes it, I think, licking the bitter grapefruit juices from my fingers.

I open the fridge and take out a loaf of rye bread; a plump, slightly green tomato; six large, brown eggs; German sausages; and a package of fresh bacon. I had gone to the market the previous evening to purchase these items for the occasion.

Closing the refrigerator door, my eyes inadvertently move to the yellow paper taped to the top right-hand corner of the fridge. I read my husband's neat slanted handwriting:

Honey, I know you'll be at work when the kids and I arrive from Vancouver, but here are the flight details:

June 23ʳᵈ
Heathrow, 8:33 am.
Flight...

The phone rings before I can finish the note.

Startled, I drop an egg. It shatters. Bright yellow yolk seeps across the gleaming floor.

I hesitate for a moment, but then pick up the phone from its cradle.

"Hello?...Oh, hi, Mum...Aw, Mum, why did you ring me there?...No, I told you yesterday that I won't be going to work today, remember?...What?...Lunch? No, can't...Why? Mum, because I can't...*Yes*, today is the day...Yes, eighteen years...Please, don't apologize for forgetting...Come down? No, Mum, don't come over. I've got everything under control...Look, I can't talk, my breakfast's burning. I gotta go...Uh huh, I know...Okay, bye, Mum."

I place the receiver down, and sigh loudly.

"And in international news, a tragic rail derailment in the Indian state of Bihar early this morning has left hundreds killed, and thousands injured..."

I turn off the tele and turn on the radio sitting on top of the refrigerator. I feel like music, something to make me dance. I turn the knob of the ancient device to my favorite radio station.

Oldies but goodies.

Humming to the music, I quickly wipe the mess off the floor. I crack the shells of my remaining five eggs, and pour the yolk into a bowl with a flare that would make Jamie Oliver blush. I rapidly beat the eggs, adding diced tomatoes and black pepper.

I ignite the stove burner with a match, adjust the hissing blue flame, and add vegetable oil to the frying pan. David prefers artery-clogging, lip-smacking, butter, but there are some things I am unwilling to compromise on, especially when it concerns the health of my family.

I cut the loaf of rye bread, and lower two slices in the toaster. I percolate the coffee.

My eye catches a framed photograph of a very young David and I on our honeymoon in Columbia. We are embracing on top of a verdant mountaintop. The photograph brings a pleasurable smile to my face. I sway my hips as my mind replays the seductive Latino music that surrounded us during the trip. The passion David and I had shared throughout our honeymoon consumes me. I feel the heat rise in my loins from the warm, fervent memories.

The popping and cracking from the heated vegetable oil focuses my attention back on breakfast.

I look around with embarrassment, and hope Mrs. Wildes is not watching me through the window.

Cheeks blushing and giggling, I pour the eggs from the bowl into the frying pan.

I set the table for four, making sure I use the plastic *G.I. Joe* plate that Harry loves, and the plastic *Transformers* plate that Daniel adores. I intermittently check the cooking food as I decorate the table with flaky jumbo croissants, orange marmalade, boxes of cereal with colorful characters emblazoned on the cardboard, a bottle of tomato sauce, glasses of chilled milk, steaming Columbian coffee, and freshly squeezed orange juice.

A reminiscent smile spreads across my face as the Beatles begin singing 'All You Need is Love' over the radio.

I sigh nostalgically.

The bubbling eggs and the kitchen dissipate as my mind travels back in time to when I had first heard that wonderful song.

Glorious sunshine and the beauty of Hyde Park suddenly surround me.

I smile coyly as David hands me a glass of wine. The French Chardonnay is beginning to make me feel bubbly, vanquishing my inhibitions.

As we enjoy our picnic at the edge of the Serpentine, I admire the boats dotting the shimmering surface and the laughing children splashing rambunctiously in the lake.

I tear a piece of bread and toss it at the dozens of quacking ducks congregating nearby. As the piece of bread hits the water, the ducks aggressively swarm and consume it greedily.

A young man, his fedora covering his face, sleeps soundly underneath a nearby willow, as the Beatles sing from his portable radio.

"Honey, I love you," David tells me while he tenderly holds my hands.

I stare at the man that has given me nothing but happiness from the moment I met him. I can feel the warmth emanating from my flushed face. I begin to get lost in his intense blue eyes. Like a warm blanket, I am embraced by his love.

"Will you marry me?" he asks.

He pulls out a ring that dazzles in the sunshine.

The smell of something burning transports me back to the kitchen.

The toast!

"Blimey!" I cry out as I extract two charred slices of bread from the toaster.

Coughing, I dump the smoking pieces into the garbage.

I glance uneasily at the clock on the microwave.

7:36 a.m.

I insert two new pieces of bread into the toaster, and throw strips of bacon and sausages into another pan, concentrating on preparing breakfast unburned and on time.

I scramble the eggs, and flip the bacon and sausages. Another pair of toast pops from the toaster. I fill a large platter with the steaming food, and hum to the radio as I bring the rest of breakfast to the kitchen table.

After covering the eggs, bacon, sausages and toast with a plastic lid to keep them warm, I step back to admire my handiwork.

A breakfast for champions, I think proudly, nodding with satisfied approval at my culinary prowess.

Filling the kitchen sink with warm water and soap, I throw the pans in to soak. I quickly tidy the rest of the kitchen, conscious of the time.

When I am finished scrubbing the pans and draining the sink, I glance uneasily at the clock on the microwave.

Shit, it's nearly 8:00. Not much time.

I open the foyer closet where I hid David's anniversary present. Grunting, I manage to drag the new golf clubs into the living room.

As the kitchen is my domain, the living room

41

belongs to David. Nothing brings him greater pleasure than to sit by the fireplace, his legs propped up, and read the newspaper. I always hear him complain about the stock market, the antiquated British fascination with the Monarchy, and the deterioration of the streets of London. He often threatens to move us into the country, although I know he loves the vibrant capital too much to act on such thoughts.

I admire the golf clubs, knowing he will love them. I know they are extravagant, but I couldn't restrain myself. When I had seen the golf clubs at Harrods I knew they were perfect for David. For far too long he had grumbled about the old, rusting set of clubs he inherited from his father. These clubs had not even been on sale, but I could not resist purchasing them. The delighted look of surprise on his face when he saw them would be priceless—a look I planned to capture on film.

I rush back into the foyer to get the other gifts in the closet. Swept up in the excitement of the moment, I had bought presents for Harry and Daniel to ensure they did not feel excluded from the celebrations.

My brow creases as I wonder whether Daniel especially will like his gift, a motorized train set I spent hours searching for.

Daniel had left for Vancouver without kissing and hugging me goodbye, cross that I had forbid him from packing his toys in his suitcase. I had angrily told him that he was too old for toys, an overreaction stemming from a terrible headache I was suffering from that day.

"Come and give me a kiss and hug before you go, Danny."

"No."

"Say goodbye to your mother, Daniel."

"Mummy is sorry, Danny. Just one quick hug."

"No, I hate you!"

"Danny, please come back!"

"Don't worry, love. He'll be missing you before we reach Heathrow."

The memory leaves me shaken. I know my son. He is stubborn, like me, and I hope my little token is enough for him to forgive me and abandon any grudges he may have. I know I am bribing his affection, but I feel guilty for my unreasonable behavior. I long to have his little arms embrace me.

Placing the elaborately wrapped presents on the living room table, my eyes catch the family portrait hanging over the fireplace. I approach the golden-framed photograph that dominates the room.

With the sleeve of my robe, I gently brush the dust off the glass.

I step back and admire my beloved family.

I recollect how much trouble and time it had been to get that picture taken. David had protested about taking an afternoon off work, and Harry was in a particularly foul mood that day. It had taken an hour to coax and entice him to wear a suit and brush his hair to a fine luster. Harry's negative demeanor had been contagious, and Daniel too began to sulk and whine about wearing a tie and stiff collar. But after the photograph, we all went for fish and chips. We laughed at how distinguished we looked in the tacky surroundings of the fast food restaurant.

I anxiously inspect the living room and kitchen one last time to ensure everything is perfect. I turn off the radio.

Everything is exactly the way it should be, I think, rubbing my hands.

In my bedroom, I hurriedly open my closet and

pull out a flower printed, cream-colored summer dress that I had dry-cleaned last week. I had worn this dress exactly eighteen years ago. Although it is simple and plain, I know it is David's favourite colour and designed in a fashion that has remained in style over the years.

I drop the dress on the bed, and walk into the bathroom. I whistle the last song that played on the radio.

Turning on the shower, I gingerly test the water with my hand until the temperature is right. I take off my robe and nightgown, and step carefully into the stall, cautious not to slip.

I sigh with pleasure as the blast of hot water hits me. As I lather my long hair, I check off my mental list to ensure I have not forgotten to do anything. Merry notes still blow from my pursed lips.

I step out of the shower and quickly dry and cover myself with a large towel.

As I walk back into the bedroom, I pause to relish the smells of breakfast wafting from the kitchen. I rub my stomach as it grumbles.

Not long now, I think.

I check the clock on the bedside table to confirm my suspicions. The display reveals that I have ten minutes.

I remove the plastic covering my dress, inspect it meticulously, and frown with disapproval as I pick off a piece of lint. Satisfied that the dress is fit to wear, I remove the towel covering me and put on a clean pair of panties. I am pleased that the dress still fits.

I put on my gold wristwatch, a gift from my children for Mother's Day. Opening my jewelry box, I pick up the elegant pearl necklace that David gave me on our tenth anniversary. I clasp it around my neck.

Standing in front of the dresser mirror, I brush my wet hair and apply lipstick.

It's nearly time.

Fingering my wedding ring, I fondly reflect on the perfect eighteen years I've had with my family. I smile wistfully as a multitude of vivid images of my children and husband flash before my mind.

My gold watch begins to beep, snapping my reverie.

It's 8:33 a.m.

I take a deep breath and pull the tiny knob on the side of my watch.

Time freezes.

The doorbell buzzes.

I try to avoid the reflection of the wrinkled face that stares back at me. I instinctively tuck a wave of silver hair behind my ear.

Closing my eyes, I visualize the note on the refrigerator.

Honey, I know you'll be at work when the kids and I arrive from Vancouver, but here are the flight details:

June 23rd
Heathrow, 8:33 am.
Air India
Flight 182

See you soon, my love.
David and the kids.

I open the dresser drawer and stare at a pile of newspaper clippings from February 11, 2003.

I randomly pick up an article and read the headline of the clipping:

INDERJIT SINGH REYAT SENTENCED TO 5 YEARS FOR MANSLAUGHTER IN AIR INDIA DISASTER

My hands shake with anguish.
The doorbell buzzes incessantly.
I select another article and scan the headline.

GREATEST MASS MURDERER IN CANADIAN HISTORY ELIGIBLE FOR PAROLE IN 20 MONTHS

Angry tears spill down my face.
This is the justice I have waited for after eighteen years? I wonder. *This is the justice that has kept me away from my family for so long?*

"No longer," I say, choking with grief as I rip every article in the drawer to shreds.

The house suddenly echoes from the desperate banging against the front door.

"It's me, dear, Mum! I know you're in there. Open up!"

Ignoring the muffled words from the front door, I lean the envelope addressed to my mother against the mirror.

I reach back into the open drawer.

"Open the door *now*! For God's sake, *please!*"

My fingers slide around the polished handle.

"See you soon, my loves," I whisper.

I press the cold barrel against my right temple.

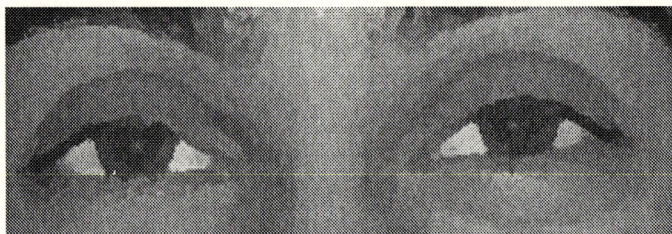

A Memorable Affair

"When you have eliminated the impossible, whatever remains, however improbable, must be the truth."

Sir Arthur Conan Doyle

Beams of sunlight crisscrossed the bottom of the swimming pool. Palm trees danced gently in the sultry breeze, seemingly moving to the song of the vibrant tropical birds hidden within its foliage. A dozen women water aerobicized in one corner of the mammoth pool, gyrating to the energetic Latino music pumping from the outdoor stereo speakers. In another end of the pool, a young Spanish couple tenderly taught their 3-year old daughter how to swim. A group of rowdy Americans lounged nearby with their hands filled with frozen daiquiris and their skin blazing red from too many hours under the relentless sun.

Standing in the shallow end of the pool, I was unaware of all of this. My attention focused on my distorted reflection.

Why? I wondered as my tears disappeared in the azure water. *I was so certain it would happen. Why didn't he—?*

My thoughts were interrupted as two arms wrapped around my waist. I forced a smile as I turned towards the man that I had fallen in love with the first time I had seen him.

His bronzed face frowned as he noticed my tears.

"Hey, what's wrong?" he asked.

Although André spoke impeccable English, he had a faint French accent that I found irresistible.

"Just sad that this is our last day in Acapulco," I said. "It's stupid, I know."

49

"No, it's sweet. Don't worry, huh? There'll be other trips," he said with a gentle smile. "Come on, focus on the positive, love. Wasn't this the perfect trip?"

I stared back at the choppy surface.

"Yeah. Perfect."

*   *   *   *   *

"So?"

"So what?" I asked evasively.

"Come on, Yvette. Tell me, did he?"

I had dreaded this moment the entire flight back to Vancouver and during the whole night as I lay in bed, unable to sleep. Even though I adored my mother and loved our weekly lunches at Marché, she was the last person I wanted to see. But, I knew my mother. If I had cancelled getting together she would have hounded me until I told her what was wrong.

I glanced around the bustling restaurant, searching for an escape.

"Well?" my mother said, bursting with excitement. "You're killing me with the suspense. Spit it out! Did he *propose?*"

"No."

"Oh my God, that's wonderful!" Mom shouted with delight. "Are you going to get married in Hawaii? Oh, I've always wanted to go to Hawaii. Your father was supposed to take me there for our honeymoon, but then your Aunt Matilda got sick, and—"

"Mom—"

"And I saw the perfect wedding dress for you the other day. It has a teal tinge to it, but trust me, you'll look stunning in it."

"Mom, please listen—"

"Yvette, what is it? Are you pregnant?"

I sighed wearily.

"No, Mom."

"Don't tell me you already got married in Mexico? You did, didn't you? Yvette, how could you do this to me? Your grandparents will be furious."

Mom stopped and gasped, her eyes wide with horror.

"Jesus Christmas Christ, what will Uncle Johnny and Aunt Gloria say? Yvette, even after *seven* years, they constantly remind me how we were their guests of honor at your cousin Doris's wedding. God, I'll be shunned by the entire family."

"Mom, no, *listen!* André *never* proposed to me."

My mother stared at me, stunned.

I was impressed. It was the first time I had ever seen her speechless.

"Mom, are you okay?"

"That *sonofabitch!*"

"Mom!"

"Forgive my language, dear, but you've been dating that ungrateful bastard for *ten* years! How can he do this to my only daughter?"

"Mom, don't say that about him. Please."

"He could at least knock you up so I could have a grandchild."

"Enough!"

My mother exhaled angrily and took out her cell phone from her purse.

"Why are you defending him, Yvette?"

"Mom, who are you calling?"

"I am going to give that French bastard a piece of my mind."

"No!"

I snatched the phone from her hand.

My mother glared at me.

"Yvette, don't you think something is terribly wrong here?"

I stared at my uneaten lunch.

"I don't know," I said.

Her expression softened and she held my hand.

"Yvette, dear, I love you with all my heart, and it pains me to say this because I know how much you love him...but, but...maybe, this is a sign. Maybe he's not the one."

I pulled my hand away from her.

"No, you're wrong, Mom. He loves me, I know it."

"Your love for him is blinding you, dear."

"No, that's not true."

"Really? Then tell me, why hasn't he proposed?"

I stared desperately at my mother, unable to answer her.

*   *   *   *   *

"André Bouchard speaking."

"Hey, hon."

"Hi, Yvette. Where are you calling from? I didn't recognize the caller ID."

"I wanted to surprise you," I said warmly. "I am calling from a pay phone just outside your office."

"Well, I'm surprised. What's up?"

"Don't tell me you forgot."

"Oh God, lunch...Yvette, listen—"

"You *did* forget."

"I'm just swamped with these depositions, love."

"Can't you get away, even for half an hour?"

"I wish I could, but I have a meeting with the partners in fifteen minutes. Hey, I'll make it up to you, I promise."

I did not reply, disappointed.

"Look, Yvette, I'm sorry. I have to run. I'll see you tonight, okay?"

"Yeah, okay."

"I love you."

"Love you, too," I said.

I hung up the phone and sighed. Reaching into my purse, I extracted my cell phone and punched the familiar phone number.

"Hi, Mom, free for lunch?...No, no, no, not Marché's...Mom, we *always* go there, let's try something different...Thai?... Yeah, that sounds good, I *love* Thai...Where's it located?...Okay, see you there in ten minutes."

*   *   *   *   *

"Aunt Gloria told me the funniest story, Yvette," Mom said as I fiddled with my Pad Thai.

"Uh huh."

We sat by the front bay window of the quaint Thai restaurant. I stared at the passing traffic as my mother spoke. Although the ambiance and food in the restaurant were delicious, my mind was still on André.

Maybe he's happy with what we share, and doesn't want anything more? I reasoned miserably. *What if he never wants to get married?*

"Aunt Gloria was having tea with your cousin, Doris, and her granddaughter, Emily, who was playing in her mother's lap," Mom continued.

"Emily is five now, right?"

"I believe so. Anyway, dear, Emily's eyes suddenly widened as she noticed that Doris had some white hair. She said: 'Mama, why do you have white hair?' to which Doris replied: 'Anytime you misbehave or make

Mama mad or sad, she gets a white hair, sweetie.'"

"That was a smart response."

I stabbed a piece of tofu with my fork. Unfortunately, I had never mastered the art of chopsticks.

"Very clever. But listen to this, Yvette. Emily looks at her grandmother and then thinks about her mother's answer for some time. Then, she says: 'Mama, why were you so mean to Grandma?'"

"Adorable," I laughed.

"Wasn't it? You know, dear, when you were a little girl..."

My eyes widened with surprise as I looked out the window.

Across the street, André emerged from an Italian bistro with a gorgeous blonde in a tight, fiery red dress. André was laughing as the stunning blonde unlocked the door to her silver Porsche parked in front of the bistro. He got into the passenger side as the roof of the sports car automatically lowered and was swallowed into the compartment behind the leather seats. The engine roared to life and the convertible tore down the street, the woman's long, blond hair blowing in the wind.

I felt like my heart had been torn from my chest and I had been punched in the stomach. I was devastated.

I dropped my fork and bent over with pain.

"Are you okay, dear?" Mom asked.

"Yeah, just swallowed something really spicy," I said, my mother's concerned face blurring from my tears. "My stomach is burning."

"I told that idiot waiter not to make the food too spicy," my mother said.

It must be a mistake, I thought with dismay. *He would never do this to me.*

But then, why did he lie to you about lunch?

another voice within me demanded.

"Here, have some water," Mom said.

She handing me a glass of tepid water.

"Thanks."

I decided not to tell her what had happened. My mother was already upset with André, and I didn't want to make matters worse until I knew for sure what was happening.

I emptied the glass with a shaking hand.

*   *   *   *   *

I carefully removed André's arm off me. His snoring ceased and I froze. I sighed quietly as his snoring resumed. I gently rolled out of bed, careful not to make a sound. I walked to the dresser and snatched his wallet.

All night I had been lying in bed, wide-awake, trying to reason what I had witnessed earlier that day. I had come to the conclusion that it must have been an unexpected business lunch. And if that were the case, then he would have purchased lunch with his corporate American Express card. All I needed was the receipt to prove it and ease my concern.

Entering the bathroom, I locked the door, his wallet clutched in my hand.

I hesitated for a moment. A flash of guilt struck me for not trusting André. He had been my best friend and lover for ten years. Could I violate the unspoken bond we shared by going through his personal items?

An image of the blonde's beaming face and golden hair shimmering in the bright sunshine filled my mind.

My nostrils flared with anger.

I opened the wallet.

Come on, come on, where is it?

I exhaled with relief as I noticed the credit card receipt tucked away in the inner pocket of the wallet.

We may not be married, hon, but after all these years I know your habits, I thought with a smile.

I unfolded the receipt and paled.

He had not used his corporate American Express card after all, but his personal Visa card. And he paid for the full amount, which had included a bottle of red wine.

This can't be happening, I thought as waves of nausea seized me. *There has to be a logical reason for this.*

I went through the rest of André's wallet, but found nothing unusual.

Tomorrow's our tenth anniversary. I'll make dinner and ask him. He'll tell me what happened and it'll make perfect sense. We'll laugh about this silly misunderstanding.

I nodded with resolve. It was a good plan. There was no need to panic and jump to conclusions until I heard his side of the story.

I returned the wallet to the dresser and got back into bed, condemned to lie awake with my troubled thoughts until the brushes of dawn etched the sky.

*   *   *   *   *

I stared mesmerized at the motes of floating dust glittering like jewels in the sunlight streaming through the kitchen window.

Although a part of me felt the warmth of the coffee mug cradled between my hands and heard the familiar sounds of André running around in the bedroom and washroom as he got ready for work, I felt remarkably calm and detached. Only the suspended flecks of shimmering dust warranted my attention. Everything else seemed insignificant.

I'm a rock, solid and at harmony with my surroundings. Nothing can disrupt my peace.

My delicate Zen-like state shattered as soon as I saw André's striking face enter the kitchen.

"Morning, love," he said.

He leaned down and gave me a kiss.

His soft lips and seductive, subtle hint of cologne melted my doubts and evoked a smile.

What am I worrying about? He loves me. Relax, Yvette. It's your ten-year anniversary with this wonderful man. Enjoy the day.

I admired how handsome he looked in his navy blazer.

"What time will you be home?" I asked.

André grabbed a piece of toast from the toaster and smothered it with strawberry jam.

"I'll be in court all day, so seven o'clock, latest."

"Okay."

I waited with anticipation for him to wish me a happy anniversary. Every year, whether it was writing me a poem or whisking me away for a weekend getaway, he had always done something incredibly romantic. I was suddenly filled with excitement at what astonishing surprise he had planned for me today.

André glanced at his wristwatch and frowned.

"Shit, is *that* the time? I have to go."

I watched with surprise as he rushed out of the kitchen.

"Have a good day, love," he said from the foyer.

The front door slammed shut.

"Happy anniversary," I whispered to the empty condominium.

    *   *   *   *   *

With my elbows on the polished dark oak dining table and my hands holding up my face, I glared at the dwindling candles with growing anger.

It was already quarter to eight, and my rack of lamb, garlic baked potatoes, and pumpkin pie had cooled and hardened.

At least the spinach salad can be salvaged, I reasoned, although I didn't feel any better.

I sat up and uncorked a 1999 Sassicaia, which André and I had brought from Tuscany last year. I took a swig from the bottle and told myself not to cry. I cursed my stupidity for spending two hundred dollars earlier that day on a sexy piece of silky lingerie. It now lay on my bed, the likelihood of it remaining untouched by André growing exponentially with each passing moment.

The grandfather clock in the foyer chimed eight times.

I stood up, smoothed the low cut, black dress André had bought me from Paris last year, and picked up the cordless phone. I dialed his cell number.

The familiar ring of André's cell phone came from the foyer.

My heart leapt with joy.

He's here!

I ran into the foyer. It was empty. His cell phone and deposition files sat on the crescent shaped table by the front door.

Feeling utterly lost, I stared at his cell phone with despair.

Disturbing thoughts of André with the blond consumed me.

I was startled as the cordless phone in my hand rang.

"H-Hello?"

"Hello, love, it's me."

"André, *where* are you?" I demanded.

"In the car."

"Where have you been? You were supposed to be home an hour ago."

"I know. Judge Turner requested my audience in his chambers and the meeting went way over."

"Oh."

I relaxed and felt ridiculous for overreacting.

"Okay, I'll warm up dinner," I said.

"Look, love, I'm sorry, but don't bother. I'm heading to the office."

"What?"

"I was going to come home, but I can't find my cell phone or my deposition files. I had to borrow a colleague's cell and my files aren't in my briefcase. The day has been a total disaster. I *need* those files tonight, and I think I might have left them in the office."

"André, your files are here."

"What was that? I just drove into a tunnel and can't hear you."

"André? Hello? Can you hear me now?" I shouted.

"What? Listen, Yvette, if I can't find those files then I'll have to re-write them tonight."

"André? Hello? What's the phone number to the cell you have? I'll call you back. Hello? André?"

"Sorry, what did you say? I gotta run, love, but I'll call you in a few hours. Bye."

I cursed as the line was disconnected.

There was no way I was going to ruin our anniversary with André working unnecessarily all night in his office. If we couldn't enjoy our anniversary at home, then I was going to make sure we celebrated our anniversary at his office.

I grabbed the deposition files, the car keys, a bottle of wine, and rushed out of the condominium.

*   *   *   *   *

Tears of betrayal streamed down my face as I stared at the silver convertible Porsche parked outside André's townhouse-style office complex.

Ten years...I wasted ten goddamn years of my life. And that bastard is fucking that whore on our anniversary. How could he be so insensitive? How could I be so blind?

I angrily brushed the tears from my face, opened the door to my car, and crossed the empty street.

André's little secret party was over. I was going to cut off his dick and throw it at his fucking lying face. Oh, he was going to suffer for the anguish he had caused me.

Unlocking the front door to the office—André had given me a set of keys to the office many years ago—I walked in the darkness past the reception area and the boardroom. At one end of the hallway, a line of light shined beneath the door.

I crashed opened the door to André's office and gasped.

"Surprise!" shouted a group of people.

The office was filled with my friends and family.

I stared at disbelief at my grinning mother. Beside her was the gorgeous blond.

Oh my God!

My eyes widened as I recognized the smiling, tanned face that had dotted several local magazine covers.

That's Francesca De Luca, the city's most renowned planner of—.

"Yvette?"

I turned around and began to cry.

Dressed in a tuxedo, his eyes sparkling with tears, André was on his knee holding a brilliant diamond ring up to me.

"Will you marry me?"

Apathy
&
Cynicism

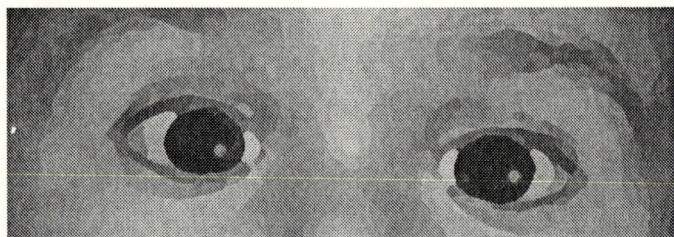

Sesame Street

*"The opposite of love is not hate,
it's indifference."*

Elie Wiesel

The little boy burst out of his bedroom and dashed into the messy kitchen where his mother was lighting a cigarette.

He tugged his mother's frayed pants.

"Mama, Sesame Street, Sesame Street!"

"What is it, Tyler?" she said.

She yawned as she flipped the page of the *National Enquirer*.

She disregarded the pile of dirty dishes and crusted pots and pans that cluttered the sink and countertop. Her thoughts remained on the bag of colorful pills taped to the back of the toilet tank. She couldn't wait until her son went to bed so she could get high. She was only in her mid-twenties but pregnancy and years of drugs, liquor, and smoking had withered her body, aged her face, and dulled her mind.

"Sesame Street time," Tyler said, his eyes sparkling with anticipation.

"Jesus, can't I get any time to myself?" she muttered underneath her breath.

She sucked deeply on the filter of the cigarette, and forcefully stubbed her butt into an empty glass beside her.

"Okay," she said to her son as she stood up from the kitchen table.

Tyler laughed with delight. He ran into the family room behind his mother.

She grabbed the remote control from the couch, and clicked on the 18-inch television.

Other than her son, the television was the only thing she had inherited from her ex-boyfriend, Hank, who had abandoned her after knocking her up in the back of his pick-up truck.

That coward prick, she thought as she flipped to the right channel.

The little boy clapped his hands with excitement as the image of Oscar the Grouch complaining to Elmo emerged.

"Elmo, Mama, Elmo!"

"Uh huh."

She returned to the kitchen with the remote still in her hand. Noticing her shaking hands, she lit another cigarette and sucked with pleasure. Nicotine was her solace until Tyler was asleep and she could escape to the bathroom.

"It's now time to learn how to tie your shoes, boys and girls," Grover said cheerfully.

Tyler ran to the front closet, retrieved his shoes, and ran back into the family room.

He put his shoes on his feet and followed the instructions from the blue puppet to tie his shoelaces. His brow furrowed with concentration as he fumbled with the laces. Tyler constantly shifted his eyes to the television to make sure he correctly understood the directions.

Tyler squealed with delight as he managed to tie one shoe.

"Mama, Mama, I tied my shoes!"

"Uh huh, that's nice, dear," came a disinterested response from the kitchen.

Tyler's attention returned to the screen as Cookie Monster ravenously devoured a seemingly endless amount of cookies.

Absorbed with the show, Tyler did not notice the

front door crash open. His stepfather, Roy, stumbled in, a beer bottle in his hand. Tyler had grown accustomed to ruckus in the house since his mother had married Roy and moved them into the dilapidated bungalow.

"Beth, what's for dinner?" Roy shouted as he staggered into the family room.

Inheriting his father's belligerent temperament, Roy had spent his youth releasing his volatile anger on his opponents as a savvy boxer. Despite his reasonable skill in the ring, multiple concussions had forced him to retire and practice his craft on his wife.

Roy's face pent up with rage as he saw the television.

"What you watching, boy?" he demanded harshly. "You become a faggot? Turn that shit off!"

"*Noooo*, Sesame Street!" Tyler whined.

"Roy, leave him alone," Beth said.

The sound of a magazine page flipping came from the kitchen.

"You shut up!" Roy roared towards the kitchen.

He turned back to the boy.

"Did you say 'Sesame Street'? I know you're a bastard, but you a sissy too? Get the hell out of here," he snarled.

Roy raised his hand to slap him.

Tyler ran into his bedroom crying. He was devastated that he was unable to watch his show.

"There's no *goddamn* crying in my house!" Roy boomed.

The bedroom door slammed shut.

Roy smirked and collapsed onto the couch. He guzzled his beer and tossed the empty bottle on the grimy carpet as he belched mightily. He glanced at his magnificent paunch, scratched his grayish stubble, and cursed the heat as he wiped the sweat off his brow.

"Fucking retard show," he muttered as Big Bird danced with a group of children.

Roy realized it was time for the football game he had wagered twenty dollars on. He grunted with frustration as he searched for the remote control.

"Beth, where's the goddamn remote?!"

Roy peeled himself off the couch and staggered into the kitchen.

"Beth!"

Beth did not reply. She read her magazine and puffed her cigarette.

"You deaf, woman? I asked you a question!"

"Can't you watch your fucking language in front of my son," she said, glaring at him. "He's only three, you know?"

"Be grateful that brat has a place to stay."

Roy opened the fridge and uncapped a bottle of beer with his calloused hand.

She stared at him with disgust as he emptied the bottle with one swig.

"Where's dinner?" he asked.

Beth turned back to her magazine.

"Make it yourself, Roy. I'm not your damn slave."

"What did you say?" he asked, his eyes narrowing. "You're living in *my* house! I provide for you and your bastard son! Now, you move your lazy ass and make me some fucking food!"

He snatched the magazine from her hands and tore it in half.

Beth stood up angrily and faced him.

"Provide? We've been living off food stamps for weeks. Provide, you say? Ha! You've been providing *shit* since you got canned last month from the factory. Jesus, look at the *shit hole* we live in."

Roy roughly pushed her towards the oven.

Beth crashed against the stove.

Pots and pans clattered to the floor.

"You shut your trap, woman. Make me something to eat. You hear?"

He turned to walk out of the kitchen.

"Here's your *fucking* remote!" she screamed.

Beth snatched the remote from the kitchen table and threw it at his head.

The remote missed Roy by an inch, and smashed against the kitchen door. It shattered into pieces.

Roy turned, furious.

"You'd still be a ragged whore if I hadn't got you off the streets. I'll have some *respect*, dammit!"

"Respect? *Respect?* Hank may have been a coward, but at least he was man enough to earn a living rather than begging for a few bucks from his pensioner mother, you drunken pig!"

Roy clenched his fists. His eyes blazed with fury.

Beth paled as she recognized the dangerous look on his face.

"Y-You stay away from me, Roy," Beth said with terror. "Stay away, or I'll call the cops."

Roy grabbed her by the shoulders and heaved her into the family room. She fell heavily onto the grimy carpet.

She scrambled onto her feet, but he was too fast. He grasped her by the hair.

"Help me! Help me!" she cried in pain.

She feebly struck his chest with her fists.

"Shut up, *bitch!*" Roy shouted.

He smashed his empty beer bottle against the side of her head.

The bottle shattered against her skull.

Beth collapsed onto the ground, unconscious.

"You'll *respect* me!"

Roy punched his fist through the drywall.

Oblivious to his bloodied hand, he stormed out of the bungalow.

The car door slammed shut. The engine caught. Tires screeched against the pavement.

Tyler's bedroom door opened a crack. He strained to hear any sound of his stepfather. Once he was certain that Roy was gone, he emerged from his room and crept into the family room. He saw his mother on the floor and approached her.

"Mama?"

He gently shook her shoulder.

She did not move. Blood oozed down the side of her face. Pieces of brown glass embedded in her flesh glinted from the family room light.

"Rubber ducky, you're *the one!"* Ernie sang, a perpetual smile on his round, orange face.

The boy glanced at the television.

Sesame Street was still on!

"You make bath-time so *much fun!"*

The puppet playfully squeezed the yellow plastic duck in the bathtub.

Tyler stepped over his mother, careful not to touch the growing pool of dark blood.

Sitting cross-legged on the carpet, he stared engrossed at the vibrant, flickering images on the screen.

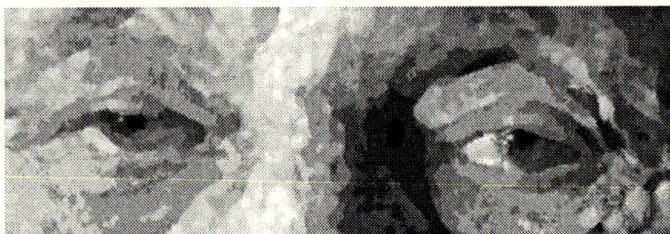

My Legacy

Science may have found a cure for most evils,
but it has found no remedy for the worst
of them all—the apathy of human beings.

Helen Keller

Ilay on my bed. The only light in the living room emanates from the muted television playing the movie *Of Mice and Men.*

I listen as my three sons—Michael, 27, Robert, 25, and Chip, 19—argue heatedly in the kitchen. Although I cannot decipher exactly what they are saying, I understand they are arguing over which one of them will take care of me tonight. Each brother tries to guilt and force the other to take on the responsibility.

My beautiful wife died when Chip was still an infant, and I had totally dedicated my life to raise my children. During those years, we had experienced our share of disagreements, and I could have been more patient and lenient, but God knew I had tried. I had spent every evening cooking and helping my sons with their homework. My weekends were dedicated to taking my boys to basketball games or the movies. I had supported any endeavor they had pursued, and allowed them to discover the beauties and challenges of life. Not once had I dated or considered re-marriage, even though I had experienced many nights of painful loneliness where I yearned for the company and warmth of a companion.

I had put all my time and energy into my boys, and now none of those sacrifices are appreciated or remembered.

When my wife had died so suddenly, it had been a difficult shock and tragic loss for all of us. But, in time, we had grieved and managed to move on with our lives.

Yet unlike my wife, I wither slowly. I live far beyond the average life expectancy the specialists predicted. I live long past the time my sons have mourned for me. I have become an inconvenience that prevents them from receiving the inheritance they have already begun expending.

The angry voices from the kitchen die down. I know Robert has lost the battle. He is the weakest of my sons, afraid of everything, especially the wrath of his two more selfish and commandeering brothers.

"Hi, Dad!" exclaims Michael as he enters the living room, which now serves as my bedroom.

When I was forced to move to the living room Michael reasoned that it was for *my* well being, as I could no longer navigate the staircase even with assistance. But I suspect this move was strictly motivated to allow Michael to return home and take over the vacated master bedroom.

Michael explains to anyone who will listen that he has nobly returned home to take care of his father and tend to the affairs of the family. But I know my son, and I am painfully aware that he was evicted from his house by the bank due to massive debts accumulated from his doomed Internet business and gambling binges. Michael has no concept of financial planning, and no control over his spending habits.

Now my conniving eldest son has a roof over his head *and* manages all my finances.

Michael speaks to me in a tone reminiscent of how a mother speaks to her infant.

"How are you, Dad?" Michael asks with a broad smile, taking my stiff hand into his. "You look *so* handsome today! Did you enjoy your lunch? I love you so much, Dad!"

My cancer-riddled brain has crippled my body and rendered me virtually paralyzed. I can only communicate through semi-coherent grunting. As a result of my dire state, I am treated and spoken to as if I was mentally challenged. But I see and understand everything. My mind is imprisoned in my incapacitated body.

"Come on, Dad, open your eyes. Come on, you can do it! That's it! *Good,* Dad!"

I cringe at the revolting sight of my beaming eldest son. I pray to God to advance the malignant tumor so it can reach my occipital lobe and render me blind.

I turn slowly to the flickering television and observe a few scenes from the movie. I enviously watch the large and dim-witted Lennie. I yearn to be Lennie, too ignorant and simple-minded to understand anything in the world. I wish to simply relish each moment, existing to be.

"Dad, we are all going to take care of you now," Michael says, slowly enunciating each word and syllable.

His face is only inches from mine. His breath smells of my $900 bottle of Dom Perignon.

"Are you still angry, Dad? Come on. There is no need for that cranky look. You don't need a private nurse to take care of you. *I* am here to take care of you, and not some stranger with shady credentials."

I glare at Michael. My piercing stare fails to penetrate the ice that encases his shriveled heart.

Not only did he fire my private nurse as soon as he discovered how much it was costing his inheritance, but he also began celebrating her departure with my most expensive champagne. It sickens me how Michael's only love is for the additional thousands of dollars he has gained by releasing the wonderful warm woman that so diligently and sympathetically tended to my needs for the past four months.

I realize with horrifying humiliation that I have soiled my bed.

Michael fails to mask the look of disgust as he catches the foul odor.

I wonder with curious satisfaction if my 'noble' son will perform the cleaning duties himself or try to evade responsibility. Either way, I hope he appreciates the critical role my full-time nurse played, especially in allowing my sons to avoid the unpleasant duties of caring for me.

"Oh Dad, did you just poo-poo?" Michael laughs hollowly as he wrinkles his nose.

His brow creases as he thinks of how to escape.

"Let's get you cleaned up, shall we?"

Michael disappears to find Robert.

I notice the light of the telephone turn red. My youngest son Chip is on the phone.

It must be six o'clock, I think.

For the next three hours I know Chip will be on the phone, speaking to his friends about the latest music, movies, and gossip until he goes out partying for the night.

Much to my chagrin, I see glimpses of Chip four times a day.

I see him in the morning when he runs past the living room to the front door heading for school. He yells for me to have a good day, his agonizing rap music blaring from his headphones.

I see Chip a second time late afternoon when he returns from school and darts past the living room. He asks how my day was, although he is upstairs in his bedroom before I can manage to grunt a reply.

I see him when he leaves every evening claiming he is going to the library. He no longer bothers to carry a book as a prop. It tarnishes the suave image he creates with his slicked gelled black hair, fine silk shirt, and crisply ironed dress pants.

I see Chip a fourth time when he sneaks past the living room around four in the morning, giggling in a drunken stupor. His gelled hair and fancy clothes are in disarray. His silk shirt is often stained and reeks of vomit.

I try to rationalize the behavior of my youngest son. Chip is either consuming his time between friends, school, and partying as a form of denial to escape dealing with my impending demise, or, more likely, he just doesn't give a damn, completely disengaged.

Robert walks into the living room. His eyes are on the floor.

"You wanted to see me, Dad?" he asks softly.

"Mmmmyyyykkkkkllll?" I grunt with much strain and effort.

"He said he was going to the pharmacy to get your medication, Dad," Robert says, still standing at the periphery of the living room.

As if on cue, I hear the powerful eight-cylinder engine of Michael's new German sports car rumble to life from the garage. I feel the vibrations of the car stereo's booming music. The convertible pulls out of the driveway and tears down the quiet residential neighborhood.

I glance at the side table beside my bed where a dozen bottles of medication are full. As her final duty, my devoted nurse had made certain my medications were restocked before wishing me good luck and leaving me to the mercy of my apathetic sons.

Robert's hunched, lanky silhouette shifts apprehensively by the doorway. After much reluctance, he sits down on the chair beside me. His hands remain on his lap. His eyes switch between the television and the floor.

Since discovering my illness, Robert has never touched me once, as if contact will somehow contaminate him with the disease.

He smells my mess, but makes no effort to help me or even utter a word. Instead, he sits beside me squirming uncomfortably in a futile effort to ease his own tormented conscience.

Robert is the only one of my sons who spends any considerable amount of time with me. But I feel no gratitude. I know his actions are motivated by his own selfish reasons.

Robert is the only religious member of the family. He embraced Christianity with zeal a decade earlier. But rather than focusing on the virtues of kindness and compassion that are preached in the scriptures, Robert is consumed with fear and guilt that he will be judged and condemned by God if he fails to fulfill his obligation to tend to his terminally ill father. And to Robert, 'tend to' means sitting silently by my side as I lie in my own shit.

Catching Robert's eye, I see only pity and fear.

I close my eyes, but do not shed a tear. I am beyond tears.

I find it ironic that such a religious man like my son advocates that death is the beginning of a new and wonderful existence with God in Heaven when in reality, deep down, he is petrified of death.

As my eyes gaze at the television, my mind turns to the past.

I remember that cold autumn day when I had foolishly taken my sons to my lawyer. I had just learned that my illness was terminal. Against the advice of my lawyer, I was determined to have my Last Will drawn in front of my children and read to them *before* I died. I wanted to live the remaining months by basking in the glow of their gratitude for all I had done and left for them. I was certain each would thank me for the bright promising futures I had guaranteed for them and their progeny.

As soon as my Will had been drawn and read to them, Michael had furiously accused me for not trusting him. He had recited the clause in the Will that stipulated that each of my children would only receive a fixed stipend from the estate until they were 30 years old.

Encouraged by Michael's outburst, Chip had also turned angrily on me. He accused me of treating him as a child as he pointed at the clause that prevented him from inheriting his fortune until he had graduated with a University degree.

Stunned, I had tried to reason with both of them that these clauses were only in their best interest. Neither listened. I waited for Robert to come to my defense, but he never spoke a word.

Later I had discovered from Father Anthony that Robert had promised to donate a significant portion of his inheritance to the local parish. If I could talk, I would congratulate Robert for trying to bribe the Almighty to reserve him a place in Paradise.

I cry out with alarm as I begin to have a seizure.

My entire body is encased in sweat and shakes violently.

Terrified, Robert stumbles out of his chair and runs out of the living room.

I do not know how much time passes.

Suddenly, three younger faces resembling my own hover over me.

Although exhausted, disoriented, and dehydrated, I am grateful the seizure has ended.

"Hi, Dad!" Michael says slowly, practically cooing. "You're okay, *thank* God. Everything is going to be fine. Your loving sons are here to take care of you."

Michael looks somber, but his bright eyes betray his excitement for being so close to realizing his inheritance.

Robert avoids eye contact, as if I am already a decaying carcass. His face contorts with fear and guilt. His right hand nervously fingers his cherished rosary.

Chip glares at me with contempt. My seizure has undoubtedly ruined his night of drinking and partying.

I can not bear it any further. I question God for my pointless existence. I beg my wife to forgive my utter failure in raising our children. I challenge Death to embrace me and transport me to the sea of tranquility.

I hear fading sounds and no longer see my sons standing around me.

I am back on my feet, a strong, young man again. I fondly watch my children sleep peacefully in their beds, the youngest in his crib. I wonder what sweet dreams they must be having.

My radiant wife stands by the bedroom door, illuminated with angelic light. Her divine face is filled with boundless love.

I turn and walk towards her.

A warm peace descends upon me as I am relieved from the burden of my legacy.

Identity
&
Purpose

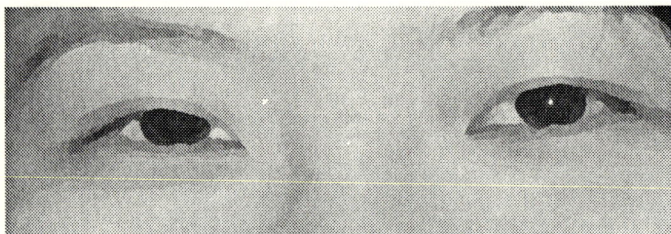

The Writer

*"We do not write because we want to;
we write because we have to."*
W. Somerset Maugham

The place is my bedroom. Many people consider their bedrooms to be a place of rest or sleep. Not I. My bedroom is something more—it is my haven.

My bedroom is large, but only holds a bed, a desk, and a chair. I need nothing more. The walls are bare and colorless, scarred by the occasional remnant of what was once there. The window that overlooks a flourishing ravine is never exposed, masked by dusty black velvet curtains.

I cherish nothing other than my privacy and my room promises me that every time I admire the radiant golden dead bolt. The engaged lock provides comfort and protection.

I am wary of what exists on the other side of the bedroom door. The door and walls are thick enough to prevent any sound from entering or leaving the room. The only disturbance comes from my mind. And although one tortured side of me screams for human contact, the other more dominating side refuses, terrified of the prospect of getting hurt—by the Truth.

This guarded fortress is my sanctuary. I command everything within these isolated walls. No one can tell me what I can or can not do. I make the rules. I do what I want.

The bed would be considered by many to be comfy. I detest it. It represents my only weakness, with its mattress and bedspread mocking me. I despise the thought of sleep. Slumber is

83

my enemy and a constant war wages between it and I. When my defenses are overcome by its onslaught, I reluctantly retreat to the mattress—apprehensive to sleep, anxious to awake.

Worse than succumbing to sleep are the dreams. When I wake up, they leave me hollow and unsettled, barely a shadow in my memory. It is my penance for being weak.

The simple wooden chair lacks any cushioning. It would be uncomfortable to most, but it perfectly nestles the length of my spine, as if customized for me. It is my throne.

The floor is cool to the touch, and provides no insulation. Its lustrous surface can faintly be seen in the dim light.

The only source of illumination is a thick wax candle. The pale flickering light barely stains the surface of the metal desk. But I am not disturbed. I prefer the darkness, which wraps around me like a snuggling blanket.

On the desk lie the instruments that provide me with purpose, the fuel that gives me the will and strength to exist: a black leather-bound notebook, a bottle of ink, and my quill.

With these tools I wantonly express all the ideas that surge and swirl restlessly in my mind. I cannot stop. I write volume after volume after volume, never looking back at my work or considering it for publication. I am satisfied by the notion that my thoughts are forever immortalized on paper.

I am a writer.

*　　*　　*　　*　　*

Lena Zhao, M.D. rubbed her aching neck as she stared blankly at the paperwork. The words began to blur, a familiar sign that she was fatigued.

She looked through the staff room window at the clock hanging over the patient-board of the Emergency Room.

Shit.

There was another three hours before her double-shift ended. It had been one of those painstakingly slow nights, where time seemed to have frozen. The most exciting case during the entire shift had been of a teenager who had accidentally jammed a Q-Tip through his eardrum.

I need an expresso, she thought. *No, a hot bath and my bed.*

A lazy smile crept across her face as she lowered her head on top of the paperwork and drifted.

"Dr. Zhao!"

"Huh?"

"We've been paging you for over 5 minutes!" Maureen Cider said.

The E.R. nurse's lips were pressed thin and her glare unsympathetic at the doctor for dozing off.

Lena wrapped her stethoscope around her neck and raced out of the staff room.

"What've we got?"

"The ambulance just pulled in," Maureen said.

The doors from the ambulance bay crashed open and the paramedics wheeled the patient in.

"We've prepared trauma room 3, doctor."

"Trauma room 3!" Lena ordered the paramedics as she chased after them. "Where's Doctor Sethi, Maureen?"

"She had to leave. Family emergency."

Lena's eyes widened as she recognized the patient

to be Mr. Hansen, her old, reclusive neighbor.

"Details?" she asked the paramedics.

"87-year-old male, complaining of chest pains. Gave him 10 of adenosine, B.P. 180 over 80."

"Mr. Hansen, can you hear me?"

Mr. Hansen was conscious, but disoriented and did not respond.

"You know this man?" Maureen asked as they stopped the gurney beside the bed.

"Okay, one...two...three, lift!" Lena said.

They lifted the patient onto the bed.

"Yeah, he's my neighbor...Mr. Hansen, can you hear me?"

"He complained of pain in his neck and arms before he collapsed," said a strange, eerily cool voice behind them.

Lena turned to face a gaunt 60-year-old man standing at the entrance of the trauma room.

"You are?"

"His son, Melvin. Is it a heart attack?"

"It's possible," she said. "Were you there when this happened?"

"Yes, I live with him."

Lena found it strange that she had never seen the man before. She pushed the thought aside. There were more pressing things to tend to.

"Maureen, let's get a complete blood count, Chem 7, blood gases, type and cross match, a cardiogram, portable chest x-ray, and...um...10 more milligrams of adenosine."

The EKG machine monitoring Mr. Hansen beeped an alarm.

"B.P. and pulse dropping fast," Maureen said.

"Shit!" Lena said.

"Father!" Melvin said sternly. "Stop this!"

"Get him out of here!" Lena cried at a young nurse standing nearby.

"Sir, you'll have to wait in the waiting room," the young nurse said.

She took his arm and led him out of the room.

Mr. Hansen's eyes fluttered open.

"M-Melvin...W-Watch him," he moaned, his frightened eyes locked with Lena.

Mr. Hansen's eyes closed.

"Mr. Hansen? Mr. Hansen? Come on, stay with me!"

"Flatline!" Maureen cried.

"Maureen, paddles! 100!"

"Charging, doctor."

"Clear!" Lena shouted.

The frail, withered body lurched forward by the electricity and fell back on the bed.

"Unresponsive, doctor."

"200, Maureen...Clear!"

Maureen shook her head. "Unresponsive."

"250!"

"Charging."

"Come on, Mr. Hansen, come on...*Clear!*"

"Faint pulse," the nurse said with a smile. "B.P. rising."

Lena sighed with relief and wiped the sweat off her brow. She handed Maureen the paddles of the defibrillation device.

"No time to celebrate yet, Maureen. We're still not out of the woods."

*   *   *   *   *

"Mr. Hansen, come with me, sir."

"Hello, Dr. Zhao," Melvin said pleasantly, standing.

He noticed Lena eyeing his black-stained fingers as she led him to a relatively empty corridor of the E.R.

"I'm a writer," he boasted proudly.

"Mr. Hansen—"

"Melvin. My father is Mr. Hansen."

"Melvin, your father is very sick."

"Yes, I understand, doctor. He gets tired easily, understandable for his age. But, we've managed."

"No, Melvin, you don't understand. He's stable but I don't know how long that'll last. Your father even stopped breathing for some time, but we revived him."

"So when can I take him home?"

Lena looked at him with surprise.

"I'm sorry, you misunderstand me. Taking your father home is not possible. Your father's heart is very weak. It has been damaged by multiple heart attacks."

"Fix it."

"What?"

"Fix it so I can take him back home."

"Melvin, your father would need extensive surgery to do so, and has declined to have any done."

"It has been a trying day for him. After a good night's rest he will see the logic of surgery."

Lena sighed wearily.

"Melvin, your father signed a D.N.R., a Do Not Resuscitate order."

Melvin's congenial expression vanished.

"There must be a mistake."

"No, there's not. He regained consciousness and was lucid for a few minutes. During that time he gave very clear instructions. He was adamant. He signed the document under his own accord and understood its contents."

"What about me?"

"Your father does not want to suffer anymore, Melvin. He yearns for a natural death without invasive medical procedures. It is our duty to respect his wishes. Can you understand that?"

"He would *never* do this to me!"

Melvin's face was filled with rage and terror. His eyes were wild and desperate.

Lena was taken aback by the ferocity and anguish of Melvin's words, but realized that dealing with the imminent death of a loved one was a difficult process.

"Mr. Han—Melvin, you must understand that your father has been quite sick for some time. Considering your father's state and age, you must have considered this possibility."

"Look, doctor, listen to me. You mustn't—can't—let this happen. Do you hear me? *Please!*"

"Melvin—"

"No! He *must* live. How will I write, *survive* without his pension checks? Tell me, *how?!*"

Lena felt as if her veins had been injected with ice water. She had heard of such people.

Mr. Hansen's ominous words came back to her: '*Melvin. Watch him.*'

Lena shivered from the old man's warning.

"I'm sorry, there is nothing I can do," she said coldly.

"No, I don't believe it. Not from a teenager playing doctor."

Lena had always been sensitive of her youthful appearance and petite figure. Despite being 32 years old, she was always asked for identification at bars, casinos or even the movies. Although she liked to look young, she hated how much her appearance adversely affected her work.

"I want another doctor!" Melvin ranted. "Someone who is old enough to make decisions."

"I can arrange that," she said with considerable restraint. "But it won't make a difference. The next time your father's heart or breathing fails we are required by law not to revive—"

"Enough! I'm checking him out."

"Melvin, I strongly advise you against such action."

"This is *my* decision to make."

"Melvin, please listen—"

"No, *no!*"

Melvin took a deep breath and tried to calm down.

"Dr. Zhao, if he's going to die, then let him die at home with me," he said, tears streaming down his pleading face. "Don't let him die in this place. He's scared here, I know he is. Let him die in peace in his home. He has taken care of me my entire life. It wasn't easy, I know. But he did, and with much pain and sacrifice. Let me take care of him now. *Please.* I can not bear being apart from him. He is all I have."

Lena stared intensely at Melvin. She finally nodded.

"Okay, fine. But your father *must* concur. Agreed?"

"Oh, yes, doctor, yes," Melvin said emotionally. "Thank you."

*   *   *   *   *

I better check the mail, Lena thought as she pulled her car into her neighborhood. She knew that a particularly lethal Visa card bill would be arriving any day now, and the thought of the interest alone was giving her gastro-intestinal discomfort.

As she pulled to the curb, she saw a familiar thin man pulling mail from one of the boxes.

"Hello, Melvin," Lena called from her car.

Melvin jumped and turned wide-eyed, like a deer caught in headlights.

"Who's there?" he asked uneasily as he shielded his eyes from the BMW's beams.

"Oh, sorry," she said.

Lena turned off the engine and got out of the car.

"It's me, Dr. Zhao."

"Hello, doctor."

"So, what are you doing up at this ungodly hour?" she asked pleasantly.

She unlocked her mailbox and frowned at all the junk mail that spilled out.

Geez, when was the last time I checked my mail? she wondered.

"Why is this hour 'ungodly,' doctor?"

"Huh...just an expression. Are you having trouble sleeping?"

"I've slept little since Father became sick. And you?"

"Late shift...again," Lena replied with a smile. "I think the head of E.R. doesn't like me. She's always giving me the worst schedules."

Melvin did not say anything, eyeing his house.

"How's your father?" she asked.

Melvin scratched the white stubble on his chin.

"Fine, considering the circumstances. He's fragile but stable. He's very brave."

"Yes, he is," Lena said, impressed.

She had not expected Mr. Hansen to live past the

night when she had tended to him a month earlier.

"That's a good sign. Look, Melvin, if you ever need me to check up on him, it'll be my pleasure. Any time, okay?"

"Thank you, doctor, but I've hired a full-time nurse to look after his needs."

"Oh? Who? I may know her."

"She just moved to the city. Listen, I better get back...."

"Of course."

Lena watched him walk away.

"Oh, Melvin?"

He stopped and turned.

"Take care of yourself," she said, concerned at how emaciated he looked. "I don't want to see you in the hospital."

He smiled.

"I will. Good night, doctor."

As Lena watched him cross the street and walk quickly into his home, she was overcome by guilt for misjudging him at the hospital.

*   *   *   *   *

With Louis Armstrong's brilliant jazz reverberating energetically throughout the jasmine-scented bathroom, Lena sighed blissfully as she slid further into the steaming water. She had been dreaming of this moment for a month, and now, finally, she had the entire weekend off to enjoy doing nothing.

Louis's cornet seized in mid-note as darkness encompassed the bathroom.

"Aw, shit."

Lena waited several minutes for the electricity to resume.

Water splashed as she carefully got out of the tub. She covered herself in a Japanese-style bathrobe she had purchased in Kyoto after graduating from medical school.

At least I can't see those five pounds I gained this month, she thought.

She peered out the window and saw that the black out had affected the entire neighborhood.

Lena fumbled throughout the house searching for any source of illumination. She found a candle without a wick and a flashlight without any batteries. When she finally did find a functional candle, she realized she neither had matches nor a lighter anywhere in the house.

"What type of E.R. doctor am I?" she muttered, disgusted at how ill prepared she was.

Lena cursed as she banged her knee making her way to the bedroom. She changed into jeans and a blouse, and walked outside where the moon radiated pale silver light across the landscape. She hated the dark—a small childhood phobia she had never completely overcome.

Lena noticed the flickering illumination of candlelight from the Hansen household.

I better see how Mr. Hansen is doing, she thought with concern.

It was a balmy evening, and she had too often witnessed the repercussions of ailing elderly suffering without air conditioning. She was sure she could help make Mr. Hansen feel more comfortable, and anything was better than sitting at home in the dark.

Lena walked up to the Hansen's front door and rang the doorbell. She tucked her wet hair behind her ears, and pressed the button again, straining to hear the bell. Nothing.

What the hell is wrong with this doorbell? she wondered.

She realized that it too ran on electricity.

Not the sharpest tool in the shed today, are we Lena?

After several moments of banging on the door without a response, Lena turned the doorknob.

The door was unlocked.

Lena hesitantly stepped inside.

"Hello? Melvin? Mr. Hansen? It's me, Dr. Zhao. Is everything alright in here?"

She was surprised that the entire first floor was completely bare, devoid of even a picture or a chair. It was as if no one lived there.

A feeling of uneasiness settled upon her.

Lena saw that the candlelight was coming from upstairs. Despite her apprehension, Lena's duty as a medical professional compelled her to move further into the house. She slowly ascended the stairs.

"Hello, Melvin? *Helllooooo!*"

Lena gasped with alarm at the top of the staircase.

The hallway was littered with black leather-bound notebooks, thousands of them piled to the ceiling. There were so many books cluttering the hallway that there was only enough space for one person to walk through.

Lena anxiously entered the gorge of paper and leather.

She paused, straining to hear a sound.

Silence.

Before her growing reservations could inhibit her curiosity, she randomly selected one notebook and opened it.

Her eyes widened at what she saw.

The handwriting was so jumbled that it was

unreadable; a never-ending trail of illegible scrawl that took up every piece of white space on every page of the notebook. The stream of nonsense words sometimes ran through other sentences—if that is what you could call them. And although undecipherable, Lena knew that this was not some foreign language. This should have been English.

Lena picked up another notebook and flipped it open. Like the previous book, every page was the same—incomprehensible.

She closed the notebook. The impulse to run was strong, but the desire to move forward stronger.

Lena warily walked into the master bedroom, the source of the candlelight.

There were books and candles everywhere. She was surprised that the entire house had not erupted into an inferno. This was a fire chief's worst nightmare.

At the end of the bedroom sat a large trunk, the only piece of furniture she had seen in the house. Candles of all shapes, sizes, and colors were strewn around it—like an altar.

Like a moth to a flame, Lena approached the trunk. After a moment of hesitation, she unclasped the latch. The feeling of dread grew.

With a trembling hand she opened the trunk.

Despite knowing what she would find, it took all her willpower not to scream.

She stared at the familiar skeletal face, the limp hair, the vacant eyes, the blue-white tinged flesh, and the withered penis.

The air reeked of sweet formaldehyde. Embalmed flesh.

Get out of here, Lena, she urged herself. *Move! Now!*

Whimpering, Lena closed the trunk.

"Hello, doctor," said a calm, cool voice behind her. "I see you've met Father."

*   *   *   *   *

"Welcome to the Sunny Creek Psychiatric Hospital, Detective Asproloupos."

The detective, who had an uncanny resemblance to a grizzly bear, enveloped the psychiatrist's lanky hand with his beefy hand.

"Dr. Lo," he rumbled. "Good of you to see me on such short notice."

Dr. Lo smiled pleasantly, unperturbed by the detective's demeanor. After studying the detective's file he knew this man was more teddy bear than grizzly.

They entered a small room that was dominated by a two-way mirror. On the other side of the mirror was an elderly man, who sat at his desk writing by candlelight. A bed was the only other piece of furniture in his room.

"Would you like some coffee?" Dr. Lo asked.

"Yeah, black, no sugar. Thanks."

The detective gestured at the subject through the two-way mirror.

"So, that's him?"

"Yes, detective."

"He remains locked up in his room all day?"

Dr. Lo handed him a steaming Styrofoam cup.

"Yes, he prefers it that way."

"Weirdo," the detective muttered under his breath. "So, Dr. Lo, tell me, straight up, no B.S. Is Melvin Hansen a murderer?"

"Melvin is no murderer," said a woman as she entered the room.

"Ah, Detective Asproloupos, let me introduce you

to Dr. Lena Zhao."

"You a shrink too?"

"No, E.R. doctor, and neighbor of the Hansen's," she said.

The policeman flipped his notepad open and nodded as he remembered.

"Oh, yes, you're the one who found the body, right?"

"That's right," Lena said.

"And what makes you think that he's not a murderer, Dr. Zhao?"

"He didn't kill me. It would have been easy. And his father was extremely ill when I tended to him. He no doubt died of natural causes. I am certain the autopsy report will verify this."

"Well, let's wait until I receive that report before we jump to any conclusions, shall we?" the detective said. "So...is Melvin insane?"

"My initial prognosis is that Mr. Hansen has phonological agraphia without alexia from a very small lesion, sub-cortical, on the angular gyrus of the left parietal lobe," Dr. Lo said.

The detective stared blankly at the psychiatrist.

"A very specific injury on Melvin's brain prevents him from writing," Lena clarified.

"And *how* did that happen?"

"The only person that knew that, detective, was his father," Lena said.

"Shit."

"But I can tell you that this is a very rare form of brain damage since in most circumstances other language-related problems, such as reading or speaking, are usually affected. This has not happened with Melvin. Only his ability to write is affected... Strange. He can't write *any* words, Dr. Lo?"

"Not one."

"Hmmm...then this brain damage must have happened *very* early in Melvin's life," Lena theorized.

"Yes, I would concur, Dr. Zhao. You see, detective, phonological agraphia prevents the patient from learning *new* words. Since Melvin cannot write *any* words, he must have had this brain trauma in his infancy before he learned to read."

"Have you seen a sample of Melvin's writing, detective?" Lena asked.

"Yeah, looks like gibberish."

"Not to him."

"Am I to understand that he has no idea of his deficiency?"

"On some subconscious level he must, but consciously, no," Dr. Lo said.

"Well, Melvin's gotta be told."

"What?" Lena said, alarmed. "Why would you do that?"

"He could be faking. This could be an act to protect himself from prosecution. Look how comfortable he looks in that room of his. Perhaps pleading insanity was his preconceived plan all along. God knows it wouldn't be the first time someone tried it."

"Thousands of volumes of writing 'gibberish' over half a century?" Lena laughed.

"Don't mock me, doctor," the detective growled.

"Detective, he's not hurting anybody and is content in his place."

"But it's not real. And it's not right, dammit."

"Who are *you* to destroy his world because of *your* notion of what is right and wrong?" Lena demanded.

"And why does it matter to *you*, Dr. Zhao?" the detective returned hotly. "Why don't you return to the E.R. and let the professionals handle this, okay?"

"I have to make sure he's okay."

"What?"

"I thought, at the hospital, his father was warning me about him. I was wrong. He knew he was dying. He wanted me to *protect* Melvin. That's all he's ever wanted for his son."

"Uh huh," Detective Asproloupos said, not understanding what she was babbling about. "So, if Melvin *truly* believes he can write like us, then he *is* insane, right?"

"Not exactly," Dr. Lo said.

Dectective Asproloupos was getting frustrated.

"Look, I don't know many *normal* people that would embalm their father and preserve his carcass like a pickle in their bedroom while assuming his identity! This mad man killed his father and took his place. Case closed."

"This is not Norman Bates, detective," Lena said. "At some level, he knows who he is, and that his father died of natural causes. He simply assumed his father's identity to outsiders to preserve his world, like he was conditioned to do."

"You mean so he could continue receiving his father's pension checks," the detective said. "*That's* his motive, doctor. Money. Nothing more. In fact, I have testimony from a Mr. Walker, a used furniture retailer, who purchased all of the furniture in Melvin's house over a week ago for $8,700."

"It is more than that, detective. Please, understand. Melvin did what he had to do to survive, and surviving meant being able to continue his writing without disruption. Not only that, he told me at the hospital that he wanted to take care of his father, like his father had taken care of him."

"Oh, Melvin certainly took *care* of him alright," the detective observed.

"Detective, Melvin has no records or any forms of identification, correct?" Lena asked.

"Yes, according to the state and federal government, this man does not exist. He has no social insurance number, medical history, license, birth certificate, credit cards, zilch."

"Amazing, isn't it, detective? But there *is* a reasonable explanation."

"Yeah? I'd love to hear it."

"Detective, as we've mentioned earlier, this man grew up without the ability to write. He can read, speak, comprehend language, but is unable to express ideas on paper."

"Yeah, so?"

"Now, writing is the one thing, the *only* thing that he wants to do. It gives him purpose. And because of his brain damage, his one passion has been denied. He's like a Mozart born deaf. Words rage in his mind, screaming to be written. Nothing else drives this man. Nothing else brings him peace."

"Do you have a point, Dr. Zhao?"

Lena glared at the policeman.

"Why do you think Melvin doesn't even know he has a problem?"

"Because no one told him?" the detective answered after a moment of thought.

"Exactly."

"How is that possible? How could his father allow him to live in such an absurd fantasy?" Detective Asproloupos asked.

"Melvin's pathology was probably condoned in order to protect him, I suspect," the psychiatrist said.

"I agree," Lena said. "Imagine detective, Melvin's

father, a man who lost his wife during his only child's birth, dedicates his life to protect Melvin from the world. He must ensure his son's happiness, even if it means locking him up and protecting him from the world for 60 years! It may have been illogical to us, but to Mr. Hansen there was no other choice. And even more remarkable, Mr. Hansen *realized* Melvin's passion and love for writing. He did everything to make sure his son continued to pursue his craft. The love and sacrifices Mr. Hansen made for his son's happiness must have been staggering."

"A touching story," the detective said dryly.

"And when his father, the man who had done everything to preserve his world died, imagine the horror and emptiness Melvin must have felt," Lena continued. "His universe, everything he knew, was precariously close to being crushed. In his mind, Melvin *had* to assume his father's place in order to protect himself, the very instinct that Mr. Hansen had conditioned in his son for decades. Hell, his father may have planned the entire thing and told Melvin to take his identity once he was gone."

Detective Asproloupos clapped brashly.

"Wonderful! Bravo, Dr. Zhao! Amazing how you put this all together without any background in investigative police work."

"Detective, this man is no violent criminal. He is suffering from pure agraphia yet believes he's a writer! How else would *you* explain it?"

"Sounds delusional to me."

"Detective, for a man of apparent intelligence your narrow-mindedness is quite alarming," Dr. Lo said.

"Now, wait a minute..."

Lena ignored the two bickering men and moved closer to the two-sided mirror. She watched Melvin hunched over his desk, his face filled with serenity.

Melvin sat up, placed another completed notebook on a nearby pile of notebooks, and opened a new notebook.

What are you writing, Melvin? Lena wondered.

On the other side of the two-way mirror, Melvin dipped his quill in the bottle of ink and started scribbling:

The place is my bedroom....

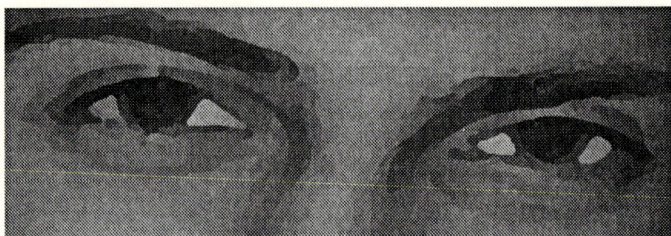

The Search

"The purpose of life is a life of purpose."
Robert Byrne

"Good morning...um...Vikram, right?" asked the shorter of the two smiling men. "Is your father home?"

I dreaded the weekly ritual of speaking with these persistent Jehovah's Witnesses. I was compelled to slam the front door on their beaming faces. But I resisted. My upbringing prohibited me from such an act of rudeness.

Or does a part of you believe that they can provide an insight to the many questions you have, a voice within my head nagged.

I had been told numerous times by friends and relatives to tell the Jehovah's Witnesses to leave, or that I wasn't interested in anything they had to say. I did neither. Instead, I warily studied each man.

I was familiar with the shorter one in the gray suit—he always came. The other man in the darker suit appeared to have a Middle Eastern ancestry. I had never seen him before, and assumed he was an apprentice.

"Sorry, but he went to work early this morning."

A tide of guilt washed over me for the lie.

The first time the Jehovah's Witnesses had come, my father had made the mistake of inviting them inside the house. They had spoken for over an hour in the living room. After that day, they had never left us alone. After dealing with them for several weeks, Papa instructed me to never tell them he was home.

I felt Papa's eyes on my back as he listened from the family room.

I suddenly found it bizarre that my parents had brainwashed me into believing that slamming the door on a stranger was rude, but lying to his face was acceptable.

The smile of the man in the gray suit faltered for an instant as he heard my words. His eyes glazed as he turned and glanced at the Saturday morning sun.

I knew he could see through my deception, but hoped he would not bring up the issue.

I grew increasingly anxious with each passing moment. In the past, he would have said, 'that's okay, we'll come back some other time,' and walked with his apprentice to the next home on the street. Now he just stood there, pensive.

Why isn't he leaving?

The man's smile widened. The sparkle in his eyes was rejuvenated as a new thought struck him.

"Vikram, how many brothers do you have?" he asked as he turned back to me.

"Two," I said stiffly.

"Yes, that's right. Two *younger* brothers, yes? There's Vijay, and you of course, and, and...?"

His brow creased with concentration as he strained to remember the name.

"Vinod," I sighed.

He snapped his fingers and smiled broadly.

"Yes, of course! And you are fifteen years old, correct?"

I nodded.

"Well, Vikram, tell me...how is the violence in your school?"

"Violence?" I echoed.

"Yes, tell me," he asked gently.

"My school is quite peaceful. I see the news and everything, but I feel perfectly safe at school."

I suddenly felt uncomfortable as I recalled a stabbing at my school that had occurred a year ago.

The Jehovah's Witness noticed my body language and leaned forward.

"Yes, Vikram, is there something else?"

"Well, we do have some fights and incidents from time to time," I said reluctantly.

The gray-suited Jehovah's Witness nodded and smiled sadly.

"The world doesn't make sense anymore, does it, Vikram?"

I remained silent.

Doesn't his face ever get tired of smiling all the time? I wondered.

"And what about *this* neighborhood?" he asked.

"What about it?"

I craned my neck to eye the oak and maple trees that dominated the serene street.

"This is a very nice place to live," I said defensively.

"Yes, yes it is, isn't it?" replied the other man with an Arabic accent. Cynicism filled his voice.

He followed my gaze with a humorless chuckle.

Although I smiled with him, his tone chilled me. I looked back at the sun-splashed neighborhood. Suddenly it seemed ominous, as if danger lurked in the shadows beneath the trees.

"Vikram," said the gray-suited man, "we go door-to-door to tell people that the world has gone bad. You know what that means, *don't* you?"

I nodded dumbly, wishing they would notice how apprehensive I felt. Couldn't they see that I wanted to be left alone? I had told them that my father wasn't home, so why wouldn't they leave?

I realized with horror that they had given up hope

on harassing Papa. *I* was their new target, still young enough to be persuaded—brainwashed.

Oh shit.

"Before, there was peace and happiness in the world, Vikram. Now there is only greed and violence."

The Jehovah's Witnesses' eyes momentarily became distant, as if he remembered how wonderful the world used to be.

I shifted uneasily as his eyes fixed upon mine— as if he was looking through me. Then, he asked the dreaded question.

"Do you believe in *God*, Vikram?"

My heartbeat thundered in my ears. My mouth was dry. I felt sweat forming along my hairline. Nausea swept through me.

I held the doorframe to steady myself.

"My family is Hindu," I quickly said, relieved at my ability to divert the question.

"Yes, of course."

Another infuriating smile.

"However, just because you were born into a Hindu family doesn't necessarily make you Hindu, *does* it, Vikram?"

I was silent. My mind raced on how to escape my growing predicament.

"Vikram," he pressed, "do you readily *practice* Hinduism?"

"Not really," I said.

I silently cursed Papa for sending me to answer the door as he sat safely on the couch. I noticed that my response seemed to please both men.

"Vikram, we believe that God is going to return to this world and fix all of man's problems."

"And not all of *woman's* problems?" I asked sarcastically.

The gray-suited man frowned. I was pleased by my minor victory.

"God is going to return harmony and love across *all* of humanity, Vikram," the Middle-Eastern apprentice said.

"Is that so?"

They nodded earnestly.

"Yes, Vikram," the gray-suited man said. "Is it alright if we leave you with something?"

No! Go away!

"Okay, I guess."

They grinned, triumphant. My acquiescence had guaranteed them the right to return the following week to discuss the material they were about to give me.

The man in the gray suit opened his worn, leather briefcase. He pulled out some pamphlets. Emblazoned on the front cover was an image of children playing in a sunny field with panda bears and butterflies.

As I reached for the pamphlets, he added: "These will help you understand, Vikram, with *scientific* proof, how God will soon return to save us."

"What proof?" I asked skeptically.

Both men shared a knowing glance.

"Well," the gray-suited man said, "read this and we can discuss it next time. Have a good day, Vikram."

They both turned and walked down the driveway.

I closed the front door and bolted it.

I glanced at the cheerful diagrams on the front of the pamphlets, debating whether or not to read the contents within them.

Papa turned on the television as I walked past the family room and into the kitchen.

My grandmother was kneading dough. She looked up and smiled at me. A streak of flour covered her right cheek.

"Who was that?" she asked cheerfully in Hindi.
"No one."
I tossed the pamphlets into the garbage.

*　　　*　　　*　　　*　　　*

That night, as I lay in bed, I had difficulty falling asleep. Usually I needed no longer than a couple of minutes before drifting into oblivion, but tonight I couldn't get my mind off the Jehovah's Witnesses.

Although I didn't believe in their words, they had forced me to re-examine the issue of God. I remembered how one day, when I was twelve, I had been playing with my toys when a thought had suddenly struck me.

Why are we here?

It was a defining moment in my life. I packed up all my toys and never looked at them again. They no longer were important. I had awoken from my blissful childhood and entered those confusing pre-teens.

I had spent countless hours struggling to determine whether or not a God existed. The debate of God and my purpose plagued me. I never found a satisfying answer, and after much time, buried those profound questions that raged through my mind. I became absorbed with the physical and emotional issues that affected all budding teenagers. I successfully had avoided those questions—until now.

For the first time in three years—as I lay in the darkness of my room and listened to the muffled symphony of crickets—I contemplated those questions I had locked away. I hoped I had enough experience and wisdom to find some answers.

So, Vikram, is there a God? I asked myself.

I was taken aback as an onslaught of other questions hit me.

Who am I?

Why do I exist?

Do I have a preordained destiny, or do I control my future?

What is my purpose in life?

For a few moments I thought about that question.

What is my purpose in life?

I repeated the question over and over again. I hoped the more I repeated it, the better chance there was of becoming enlightened.

Okay, Vikram. Reason this out, I told myself.

I unconsciously cracked my knuckles.

Okay...Well, if I assume there is a God, then we must have been put on this Earth for some purpose. And when we die, we will continue to exist through our souls. But, on the other hand, if there is no God...

I frowned.

No. I can't exist just for the sake of existing, can I?

A sense of dread filled me as I considered that possibility.

Is life simply a freak coincidence that occurred billions of years ago?

I could not accept the terrible chance that I had been created like every other human by some genetic fluke. It was too terrible to consider the possibility that once I was dead, all the knowledge, wisdom, love, and experience I had acquired would be forever gone— turned to dust.

Is such a calamity possible? Is the soul a farce, a myth created to deceive us?

I shuddered at the possibility.

No, I thought, shaking my head, *we are here for some reason, maybe for something that is beyond our comprehension, but for some reason nevertheless.*

Millions and millions of people relied on God to protect them and seek His guidance. People believed that their actions in life would dictate whether their soul was rewarded or condemned in the afterlife. They believed this because the alternative meant that life had no hope. And without hope, nothing mattered.

For most of the world where suffering was prevalent, God gave people enough strength to make life bearable.

All those people can't be wrong, can they? I wondered uneasily.

And what about all the beauty in the world? The images of the breathtaking marvel of Earth from space or the immaculate crystalline artistry of a snowflake were too beautiful to be a cosmic coincidence.

How could the glorious transformation of a caterpillar to a vibrant butterfly, or the awe-inspiring majestic splendor of a frothy waterfall in the heart of a rain forest be created other than by the imaginative genius of some divine power?

How could the creation of life, our own self-awareness, or the indestructible love a mother has for her baby be explained other than with the presence of some omnipotent force?

Sure, the media was filled with disasters and tragedy, but I also knew that countless acts of goodness happened daily throughout the world.

So there must be a God!

I was satisfied with my reasoning, and felt some burden escape me. I was making progress.

My smile dissipated as I felt a mosquito bite me. I slapped my hand against my arm.

I studied the dark blood and the crushed remains of the insect on my palm.

If God is out there to protect and watch us, then why is there so much pain, suffering, and loss in life? I wondered.

I heard my grandmother shuffle slowly past my bedroom door. I knew her arthritis was especially painful at night and going to the bathroom was an arduous task for her. Despite watching her grunt and wince from pain each day, she always smiled when she caught me looking at her. Rather than complain, God's praise would instead escape her lips.

Perhaps the suffering we endure is a test of faith. Perhaps the sacrifices we make in this life ensure we are rewarded in the next.

Another barrage of questions filled my mind: If there was a God, then *which* God was *the* God? Allah, Brahma, Buddha, or the father of Christ? Was there a blue-skinned, six-armed, crowned elephant competing for reverence with hundreds of other deities as Hinduism claimed?

Now that I believed that there was a God, which religion was the true religion to follow?

I knew the question was important. The entire world, as I knew it, was influenced by religion. Throughout history, there was no greater cause of war and death than from religious groups killing to preserve and spread their own beliefs.

I was afraid—no, terrified—that if I believed in the wrong religion then I would be damned to Hell or Purgatory or some other terrible place. Would I be punished despite lacking any control over whom I was born to? Why was I born into a Hindu family if Christianity or Buddhism or Zoroastrianism was the only true religion? Or what about that child born in the desert in Mongolia or in the frozen tundra of the Arctic, never exposed to Islam or Sikhism or any other religion? Would that child be condemned despite his or her ignorance?

If only there was a way of really knowing. I needed solid proof, and not some propaganda from a tacky pamphlet handed to me by an excessively smiley man in a cheap gray suit.

I thought of the customs in my religion. Although my grandmother was extremely religious, neither of my parents had forced us to practice our religion rigidly. I was thankful for this. It allowed me the freedom to believe what I wanted to, without any preconceived notions. My parents had given me the free will to explore and discover the world on my own. I was encouraged to embrace whatever faith best fit my own values. Sure, I was utterly confused at the moment, but I still appreciated the right to exercise my choice.

What about those who don't have a choice?

I wondered about those children who were forced to practice their religion. If they didn't acknowledge God's existence every Sunday, or pray every time they ate, would they be damned? If you were a Muslim, but one day ate a pepperoni pizza, were you condemned eternally? What about a Hindu that feasted on a piece of beef tenderloin, despite knowing that cows are revered and sacred? Say if Christianity was *the* right religion, then did a non-practicing Christian have a better chance of entering Heaven than a practicing Jew? And what about Protestants and Catholics? Why were they killing each other in Northern Ireland when they were *both* Christians?

Nothing made sense to me.

My head throbbed. I massaged my temples.

Everything seemed so complex and confusing.

What does your heart say, Vikram? a voice within me asked.

I shut my eyes and tried to listen to my gut instinct.

As long as you believed in *something* that was all that mattered.

Having faith is the key.

Following a religious custom was not necessarily religious. True, it provided an opportunity to clear your mind and soul, but I felt it was not crucial if they were followed or practiced.

That is what my heart told me.

It seemed ridiculous to me that people dedicated so much effort to constantly pray to God for gratitude. God couldn't be so vain, could He?

I frowned. Wasn't *vanity* a deadly sin?

And how do you know if 'He' is a 'He'? Maybe 'He' is a 'She' or 'It'?

I sighed and opened my eyes. The more I searched, the more questions I confronted.

I cursed myself for throwing away those pamphlets earlier. At that moment I was prepared to settle for *any* answer to resolve my conflict.

A growing pressure in my bladder disrupted my thoughts.

I had to pee.

I waited until I heard my grandmother shut her bedroom door before I rolled out of bed with a tired groan. I made my way in the darkness to the bathroom.

Other than lying in bed in the middle of the night, sitting in the bathroom was the best place to contemplate. It was a place where I was able to completely focus my thoughts with remarkable clarity—without disruption, interference, or influence.

Forget about a pilgrimage to Mecca, Bethlehem, or the Golden Temple, I thought with a smile. *The bathroom is my temple.*

As I lowered my pajamas and sat on the cold, plastic seat, I wondered whether God was watching. I suddenly became very conscious. I nervously glanced at the darkness that encompassed me.

Another and more disturbing thought hit me.

What if God is aware of all my thoughts?

If He was omnipotent and omnipresent then it was not only possible but likely. And if that was the truth, then I was in trouble. There were numerous times I had thought of things that I was ashamed of, especially during moments of anger. I recalled with regret how only that morning I had internally cursed Papa for making me answer the door because he didn't want to deal with the Jehovah's Witnesses. True, I had later felt remorse for having such thoughts towards my father, but was that a justifiable excuse?

Perhaps words or thoughts were inconsequential, another part of me reasoned. What if only my actions were judged?

We all had moments of weakness from time to time, but our thoughts didn't hurt anyone unless we acted upon them, right? No, but what if...

Wait, what am I doing? Stop this, Vikram!

Everything was based on assumptions, I realized. I could spend my entire life in search of answers to these profound and universal questions. For centuries, sages, priests, swamis, saints, gurus, monks, imams, rabbis, all of them had dedicated their lives to find the Truth, and how successful had they been?

I'll probably be on my deathbed when I figure it out.

I chuckled. If that was the case, then God had a

very morbid sense of humor.

Perhaps, we are merely His entertainment, part of a universal soap opera, like the Greeks were to Zeus. If so, is all of this a grand joke? Is the world a stage and we His puppets? Is that our purpose, to be His stringed marionettes?

I looked out the bathroom window and admired the countless stars that blanketed the sky.

If each star represented a sun, then how many billions of planets existed in the universe? I wondered. And if there were billions of planets, the possibility of intelligent life elsewhere was not only feasible, but probable. What if there was one God that oversaw a myriad of intelligent species throughout the universe? If so, then maybe no religion on Earth was remotely close to reality, and God was some force, some greater phenomenum that transcended our comprehension. What if God was something that was responsible yet unconscious of our existence?

I sighed wearily and flushed the toilet. I could go mad thinking like this. I was going in endless circles.

As I washed my hands, I suddenly expected to hear God's comforting words telling me what to think or do and alleviate my uncertainty.

I turned off the tap, held my breath and waited to be enlightened.

"Yeah, right, Vikram," I snorted in the darkness.

I felt like a fool.

In the mirror, I studied the shape of my silhouette. I was filled with confusion and frustration.

What is the truth? I demanded at my reflection. *Tell me!*

I gasped as the rays from the waning moon suddenly illuminated my face.

Is it possible?

I leaned forward, studying my reflection.

Am I staring at the truth?

My face disappeared into darkness as the moon was covered by a cloud.

Is the answer so simple?

God existed, but *within* us. God was constantly whispering in our ears, I just had not realized it. How else could I explain that inner voice that always told me the difference between right and wrong?

God was my soul. His voice my conscience. As long as I was a good person, finding peace within myself and caring and loving others, I could not go astray.

And my purpose? I asked myself. *Well...if God's voice is my conscience then...*

Of course!

Deep down, I had always known what I wanted to do, but never had the courage to follow my dreams. I was afraid. I had justified to myself that I could never be good enough.

Why didn't I see it before? I wondered.

God had not only given me the skills to attain my dreams, but He had also urged me to do so since I could remember. The Creator had been telling me my purpose since the beginning. I had ignored His voice through the fear of failure. But now I knew it was the course towards fulfillment. As long as I listened to my conscience, I would journey down the right path.

My purpose was to focus my energies towards what I was passionate about, to excel at what I was meant to do. Through persistence, courage, and confidence, failure was not possible.

God had planted the seeds and it was up to me to nurture my passion.

I could never prove my theory, but the endless questions that burdened my mind were gone. I felt liberated. Free!

My countenance was filled with relief. I was filled with an exhausted satisfaction.

As I walked back to my bedroom, my vision became bleary with sleepiness. I yawned deeply as I got into bed. My mind was wonderfully empty.

I rested my head against my pillow. Drool collected in my mouth and trickled from my lips.

Sleep would soon be upon me. Wonderful, peaceful, sleep.

The last thing I heard before I fell asleep was my grandmother's sweet voice from the neighboring bedroom. Like every pre-dawn morning since I could remember, she was singing her daily prayers.

"Om bhur bhuvah swah...[1]"

---

[1] Om bhur bhuvah swah. Tatsavitur varenyam. Bhargo devasya dhimahi. Dhiyoyo nah prachodayat.

[1] Oh God, the Giver of Life, Remover of Pains and Sorrows, the Bestower of Happiness, and Creater of the Universe, Thou art most luminous, pure and adorable. We meditate on Thee. May Thou inspire and guide our intellect towards the path of righteousness.

Courage
&
Fear

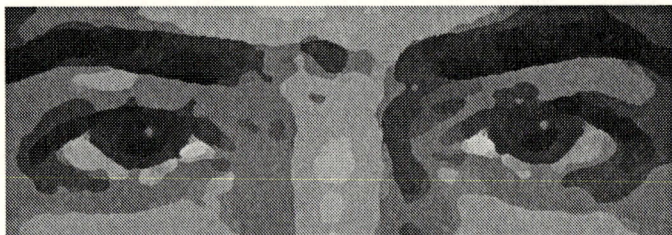

Crescent Moon

*"Cowards die many times before their deaths;
the valiant never taste death but once."*
William Shakespeare

Intoxicating—that's how I would describe the sweet perfume and opium-smoke that saturated the back of the shady hotel that served as a brothel.

A dozen men sat on lush pillows on the thick-carpeted floor, staring into blissful oblivion as alluring prostitutes dressed in enticing translucent silks draped over them. Persian music drifted as enchantingly as the hazy smoke.

I stared stoically at the imposing, bellicose figure sitting in the booth across from me.

His only eye glinted ominously. The scrunched mass of flesh where his right eye should have been and the missing lobe of his left ear accentuated his brutally scarred face. These disfigurations were permanent reminders of the atrocities he had suffered by the Russians during their occupation in Afghanistan. Now an arms trader for the Taliban, his duties included smuggling weapons and equipment to Kashmir jihadis—Islamic militants who continued to infiltrate the Line of Control into the Indian state of Kashmir.

I had dealt with this Muslim warrior over the past eighteen months, and still did not know his name. As a result, I had secretly nicknamed him 'Cyclopes,' the one-eyed monster of Greek mythology.

"The merchandise?" I asked in Urdu.

"No merchandise this time."

"Oh?"

"Special orders instead for Omar Khan."

"I don't like changes," I growled.

123

"Instructions are in the same place," Cyclopes said impassively, though his eye blazed. "Wait until I leave before you retrieve them. Understood?"

I glared at him, rigid and wary.

"*Understood?*" he said.

I nodded and emptied my drink. I slammed the thick glass on the table.

"Praise Allah—peace be with Him—and our great cause," he said.

He stood and vanished into the thickening haze of smoke.

I noticed that Cyclopes had not touched his drink.

As I discreetly removed the thick envelope taped to the underside of the table, my breath caught in my throat.

A stunning prostitute, her face resembling a porcelain doll, emerged from upstairs. Her fiery, sapphire eyes were focused on me. I had never seen her before, and was captivated by her beauty. I yearned to whisk her back upstairs to a private room.

Standing, I threw some tattered rupees on the table to cover my fare.

I hesitated and momentarily locked eyes with the beautiful prostitute again. I was magnetically drawn towards her.

It would only take a moment. No one would know, I reasoned.

I shook my head as a commanding second voice filled my mind.

No! No matter how tempting, the risk is too great.

Ignoring the burning desire in my loins, I reluctantly walked through the beaded curtain into the next room.

Pausing, I looked through the vertical strings of glittering beads.

The voluptuous woman moved towards another patron. She sat with seductive grace on the lap of a slothful man, who seemed more preoccupied smoking from his hookah than being with her. As she nuzzled his fleshy neck, she continued to stare at me.

A hint of a smile touched her lush lips.

Turning, I knocked on the hidden door that led into the hotel. Retrieving the weapons I had checked-in from the front desk, I left the dilapidated building.

My lookout appeared from the shadows from across the street and joined my side.

*   *   *   *   *

I was grateful for the cool mountain air; it cleansed my mind of the alluring prostitute that lingered in my thoughts. I admired the brilliance of the millions of stars that splattered the cloudless black sky, and at the crescent moon, a sliver of light that radiated over the precipitous landscape.

"What did Cyclopes say, Amar?" Inder asked in Hindi.

"It's *Ali,* and don't speak in Hindi," I sternly replied in Kashmiri.

"Relax, brother. We're in the middle of the mountains, miles from civilization. Only stones and trees listen here."

"And spies."

"If I can't talk to you now, when we're alone, then when?"

I glared at my older brother.

"Okay, okay, chill, man...God, when will this cursed assignment end? When I joined the army I thought I

125

would be killing terrorists, not pretending to be one!" he complained as he scratched his itchy beard.

"Will you shut up?" I hissed.

I warily studied the surroundings. The machine gun felt reassuring in my hands.

Inder thankfully fell into a sulking silence.

We turned off the winding road that snaked up the mountain and entered a dense forest.

The thick foliage, swaying gently in the evening breeze, blocked the moonlight.

We followed the indiscernible path that we had trekked a hundred times. I knew every crevice, jutting root, and stone on the path, and walked without trepidation.

With my brother's careless comments leaving my mind, I relished the soothing symphonic sounds of the night — the excited chirping of crickets rubbing their hind legs together with vigor; the melancholic hoot of a mountain owl; the hoarse croak of river frogs; the nervous scurry of mouse hares, scrambling for shelter at the sound of our approaching footsteps; and the content sighing of the rustling leaves and grass.

The charming words uttered from Moghul Emperor Shah Jahan, when he first visited Kashmir centuries ago, came to my mind.

'Agar Firdous Bar Roi Zamanast Tho Haminasto, Haminasto, Haminasto' – 'If there is a heaven on earth, then it is here, it is here, it is here.'

I wondered what Shah Jahan would have thought if he knew his heaven—once the premier destination for lovers, honeymooners, and tourists—was now fraught with danger, misery, and death.

I sighed at the irony.

As we reached a stream cutting through the forest, I paused to admire the dark water flowing peacefully downhill.

My brother trudged past me and crossed the stream. As he reached the far bank I wondered whether I had been too hard on him earlier.

Inder suddenly cursed in Hindi as he tripped over a rock. A fusillade of bullets erupted from his weapon as he hit the ground.

I dove into the water to avoid the bullets whizzing past me.

As the echo of the machine gun's discharge dissipated, I strained to listen for anything unusual, for any sign of enemy movement.

Only Inder's whimpering was heard.

I waded through the water until I reached the shore. I roughly pulled my weeping brother to his feet.

"I-I-I am sorry."

"Move, quickly!" I said, shoving him.

"I-I-It was an accident, Amar."

"It's *Ali,* dammit!"

He stood there, defeated and crying.

Staring at my brother's frightened eyes, my anger dissolved. I remembered my vow to my sister-in-law.

When I had joined the military, I had tried to dissuade Inder from following me. He felt it was his duty to kill the terrorists that threatened his country and fulfill his destiny of becoming a revered hero of India, like he watched in Bollywood films. When Nandani, my brother's newlywed pregnant wife, had failed to alter her husband's decision, she had taken me aside just before we had left for boot camp.

"Amar, I beg you, please protect Inder," she had pleaded. "He's not strong like you. Please, promise me. Promise you'll bring my husband back to me, the father of my unborn child. I can't live without him. In front of me and God—promise!"

Although reluctant to bear such a responsibility, I promised.

For the next months, I prayed that Inder would be deterred by the harsh reality of boot camp. But his positive, good nature had been oblivious to the dismal and harsh environment. As I scored first in every physical milestone during training, my brother finished last. I was certain he would be sent back home to his wife. But the Indian military was desperate to get more troops to the frontline, especially those that spoke fluent Urdu and Kashmiri. Much to my dismay, Inder passed the training.

I was certain that with time our Commanding Officer would realize the shortcomings of Inder as a Special Forces operative and assign him to a desk job in New Delhi. But, no order was given. When it came time to assign us to the frontline, I made a special request to my superiors to post Inder with me so I could keep a watch on him. Although our Commanding Officer frowned at siblings working so closely together in his unit, he had reluctantly conceded to my pleas.

Only six more months. Then Inder can be posted somewhere else that's safe or leave the army. Then my burden will be lifted, I reminded myself.

I squeezed Inder's trembling shoulder. My expression told him that everything was all right, and that I would let nothing happen to him.

Inder drew strength from my confidence and reassurance. Tightly clutching his weapon, he motioned me to lead him deeper into the woods.

*   *   *   *   *

After an hour, we entered a verdant field. The grass was as high as our waist.

On the zenith of a hill before us was a small cabin. Smoke poured from its chimney. A flickering warm yellow light burning from its windows provided the illusion that a loving family resided within its wooden walls. But I knew that the cabin's former residences had been brutally murdered. Those wooden walls now only witnessed death and blood. The cabin had become one of three-dozen safe houses for the Islamic terrorists that dotted along the Indian side of the Line of Control.

Trekking in dangerous territory, I scanned the surroundings, my guard up. I hoped our visit would be short. I wanted to deliver the message to Omar and get out.

As we approached the cabin, the red burning dots of two cigarettes glowed and flickered from the roof. The two sentries leaned casually on the chimney, their rifles pointed at us. One of the guards ordered us in Urdu to give the password.

Although I could not see him, I knew a third sentry was positioned somewhere in the periphery of the forest, hidden in the shadows. The hairs on the back of my neck tingled as I felt the gunman staring at me through his infrared rifle-scope.

Inder recited the correct password.

The sentry on the roof lowered his rifle and signaled us to pass.

I knocked on the front door.

A menacing, burly face—Aziz, Omar's personal bodyguard—replaced the weathered wood. Once he had inspected us and confiscated our machine guns, he permitted us to enter.

129

"As-salaam-alaikum, brothers," Omar said with a broad smile.

Omar Khan was one of a handful of clandestine Kashmiri separatist leaders with a large financial and military backing from Islamic fundamentalist regimes, such as the Taliban. He had been leading the separatist movement for over a decade. Despite Indian intelligence knowing his importance, New Delhi had given strict instructions to allow Omar to continue his operations until his connections were discovered and captured.

"Wa-alaykum-as-salaam," Inder and I replied.

"What news do you bring from the brothel?" Omar asked.

I gestured towards the turbaned figure sitting quietly in the shadows in one corner of the room.

"Who is this, Omar?"

"Forgive my rudeness. Ali, Mohammad, meet Islam Ahmed."

"Islam Ahmed never crosses the Line of Control," I said suspiciously, although my mind was whirling.

Islam Ahmed was one of the most wanted men in India. He had been directly linked to several terrorist bombings in Srinagar, New Delhi, and Mumbai that had killed hundreds of innocent people.

Finally, all those months of dangerous undercover work was going to pay off, I thought.

This was the opportunity I had been anxiously waiting for. Islam Ahmed was within my grasp!

I wondered how I could find a quick moment of privacy to summon my unit to capture the treacherous terrorist.

"Ah, I'm pleased my reputation precedes me," Islam Ahmed said, his face concealed in darkness. "But there is a matter I must personally oversee to ensure the success of our great cause."

"What matter?" I asked.

Aziz suddenly blocked the front door. His machine gun pointed towards us.

"That we have a traitor, an infidel spy, amongst our ranks," Islam said.

Islam stood from the shadows.

I gaped incredulously at the familiar gruesome face, the one-eye glinting dangerously at me. I was stunned that Cyclopes, the man I had met monthly over the past year-and-a-half was in fact the infamous Islam Ahmed.

How could I have missed the signs?

"*You* are Islam Ahmed?" I asked.

"Anonymity has its advantages in my business," he said.

"What traitor?" Inder asked as he glanced uneasily at me.

Islam signaled to Aziz, who grabbed Inder.

"No, Ali!" Inder cried.

"What is the meaning of this?" I demanded.

"String him up!" Islam sneered, ignoring me.

Inder glanced at me wildly. His face contorted with terror as Omar and Aziz roughly fastened his arms to the overhead wooden beam.

The survival part of my brain urged me not to panic.

"I've known this man for two years," I said with remarkable calm. "Mohammad is no traitor."

"You mean *Major* Inder Seth, don't you?"

I laughed and searched for options of escape.

"For a man that has eluded the Indians for so long, Islam, your intelligence is surprisingly flawed."

"Is it?" Islam smiled. "Tell me, Ali, what true Muslim uses whores to satisfy his lust, a major sin prohibited in the Qur'an, and strictly forbidden by Allah—peace be with Him?"

I paled and glanced at my brother, whose face was filled with guilt. He avoided my disappointed, surprised gaze, and remorsefully hung his head to conceal his tears.

I glared at Islam.

"All men succumb to weakness. Prostitution is rampant in many Muslim countries. That doesn't make him a traitor to our great cause, now does it?"

"No, but boasting to a whore that he's a spy for the Indian military does!" Islam said, his eyes wild.

"Lies!" I hissed.

"Then open the envelope I asked you to bring here," Islam said with a thin smile.

I pulled out the envelope that I had brought from the brothel and tore it open. My heart sank as an audiocassette slid into my hand.

Islam smirked.

"Shall we play it? It was recorded by a particularly enchanting woman who was doing the work of Allah—peace be with Him—while you waited for me. I believe you noticed her eyeing you once I left the brothel. While we spoke, she was with this infidel spy upstairs."

I stared at my brother with shock. How could he be so foolish!

Realizing Inder's fate was sealed, thoughts of my own escape consumed me.

"No," Inder protested, shaking his head. "*Please*, listen—"

"Silence that traitor!" Omar roared.

Aziz swung his machine gun over his shoulder and began to punch Inder.

The cabin was filled with the sound of cracking bones and wretched cries.

Save yourself, Amar, my inner voice urged as I dumbly watched Aziz beat my brother into a bloody pulp. *There is nothing you can do for Inder.*

"Enough," Islam ordered.

Aziz stepped back. His knuckles glimmered with Inder's blood.

Islam extracted a revolver and handed it to me.

"Now, kill this treacherous swine, Ali."

I stared at the revolver in my hand.

I can't kill my brother, can I?

Time froze. It felt like hours before the initial shock of what was happening began to wane.

"Have you forgotten how to use a revolver?" Islam asked, sounding like a concerned teacher encouraging a struggling pupil. "Here, let me help you."

Islam took the gun and pulled the hammer back. With a click, the hammer was locked into place.

"There you go, Ali. All you have to do is point and press the trigger. That's it, you can do it."

I had no choice. If I hesitated any longer, I would also be strung up and tortured beside my brother, as good as dead. They were still unsure whether I was trustworthy. That meant I had a chance to survive.

Inder looked at me bravely. His bloodied face was filled with acceptance, ready to embrace death.

Please don't tell Nandani the truth, his swollen eyes pleaded.

I nodded and raised the gun at my brother.

"Do it!" Omar cried. "Butcher this infidel!"

Islam hungrily licked his lips with anticipation.

Inder spat blood on me.

"Burn in hell you muslim pigs!" he screamed.

I pressed the trigger.

The empty chamber clicked.

Islam laughed—it was a chilling, hollow laugh.

Omar smiled cruelly.

I dropped the gun on the floor, devastated at what I had done.

"We weren't sure about your loyalties, Ali. You understand," Islam said as he retrieved the gun. "And we couldn't risk giving you a loaded weapon if you were disloyal, could we?"

I nodded, dazed, my eyes on my brother. Relief washed through me so strongly that I felt nauseated.

Islam stopped smiling. He sat back down in the corner of the room. His rigid, cold face vanished into the shadows.

"Omar."

Omar pulled out his own handgun and emptied eight bullets into Inder.

Blood, flesh, and muscle exploded against the back wall.

I fell to the floor and threw up.

Tears blurred my vision.

Even after my brother's dangling body went limp, the deafening discharge from the gun reverberated in my tormented mind.

"Aziz, take him outside to clear his head," Islam ordered. "Omar, cut that infidel pig down and get it out of my sight."

I felt two large hands force me to my feet. With Aziz's help, I stumbled through the cabin's back door.

The cool mountain air struck me, numbing my mind. I grasped an empty wooden barrel by the back door. Lowering my head over its opening, I heaved and wheezed.

"Death is hard to bear when it's a friend," Aziz said as he lit a cigarette. "Allah's work is difficult, but sacrifices must be made for us to enter Paradise."

My body shook violently as I pretended to throw up. With one hand I pulled my military knife from its sheath that was strapped below my right knee.

In one swift move, I covered Aziz's mouth and sliced his throat. Warm blood gushed over my hand.

I let go of the corpse and watched it slump to the ground.

Extracting my handheld radio, I punched in the emergency code to relay to my unit that I needed air support. A tracking device within my handheld radio would provide the exact co-ordinates of my location.

I took Aziz's machine gun, made sure it was loaded, and pressed my back against the cabin wall.

The two sentries on the roof laughed over some crude joke. Inside, I heard the sickening thud of my brother's carcass hit the floor as his ropes were cut.

Absolute terror suddenly seized me. I was incapacitated with fear.

What if I am caught? What will they do to me?

The sudden distant rumbling of an attack helicopter gave me focus. My support had responded far faster than I had anticipated.

I griped the machine gun tightly and stared longingly at the safety of the woods. I had to move quickly but was still paralyzed with terror.

One of the sentries barked at his comrade to be silent. Realizing a military helicopter approached them, he shouted a warning.

The sentries scrambled to their feet, loaded their weapons, and turned on a powerful searchlight.

I glanced through the cabin window and saw Omar and Islam rushing for their weapons.

Having only a few seconds to escape, I regained the use of my legs and sprinted out of the shadows.

I ran as fast as I could towards the safety of the thick foliage.

The door to the cabin crashed open and several shots were fired at my direction. Omar shouted orders at his men on the roof to kill me.

Turning to my side as I dove to the ground, I screamed as I fired several bursts towards the front door of the cabin.

Omar stumbled back from the force of my bullets and collapsed onto the porch.

A black military attack helicopter emerged from behind the ridge of the hill. Its nose down, velocity slowing, the helicopter's powerful cannons released a barrage of bullets at the sentries on the roof of the cabin.

The searchlight exploded with a bright flash.

The sentries toppled off the shattered, splintered roof.

The roar from the helicopter's turbo-shaft engines was deafening. Its whirling four-bladed rotor, like a tornado, ruthlessly blew the tall grass.

Urging myself to move, I stumbled onto my feet.

Six black clad paramilitary troopers, like ninjas, zip-lined sixty feet from the hovering aircraft. Unclipping their quick release attachments as they landed, the troops surrounded the cabin. Night vision goggles were strapped around their heads.

As I got to my feet, I suddenly remembered the other sentry hidden at the periphery of the forest.

I whirled around and stared at the rifle pointing towards me. The barrel stuck out from the darkness of the woods, the rays of the crescent moon reflected off its menacing black metal.

Before I could raise my gun there was a flash from the muzzle.

*   *   *   *   *

Consciousness returned to me with a cloud of terror. A perpetual abyss of blackness surrounded me.

From the acuity of my perceptions, I knew I was awake—I could feel the sheets of the bed against my skin, the draft from a ceiling fan above me, and the syringe in my arm sending nutrients into my vein. I could hear the beeping from a heart monitor and hushed professional voices in the background. The room smelt of disinfectant and had a faint trace of urine.

I was in a hospital, but I could not open my eyes. The darkness was so intense that I was overcome with claustrophobia.

"Hello, please help me!" I cried out in Hindi.

I tried to sit up from the hospital bed.

Someone quickly approached me. I was consumed with fear and on the verge of hysteria.

"Major Amar Seth, I am Doctor Sharma. Please, you must calm down. You're safe now."

"I can't see!"

"Yes, I know. Please, you must calm down. Otherwise we'll have to restrain and sedate you. Take deep breaths and lie down."

Gasping heavily, trying to control my panic, I lay down. I was very thirsty. I traced my parched mouth and cracked lips with my dry tongue.

"Good, that's it. Much better," Doctor Sharma said with approval.

I noticed the tightness of bandages around my head. I gingerly touched the gauze. I snapped my hand back, as if I had suddenly been burned.

"What's happened to me?" I asked, crying.

"I'm afraid you were shot," the doctor said.

As soon as he uttered those words, I noticed a dull throbbing in my left thigh.

"We were able to remove the bullet," he continued. "Fortunately there was minimal damage. None of your major arteries were struck. You'll heal completely, Major Seth. With some rehabilitation, your mobility will not be adversely affected."

"Why can't I see?"

"Ah yes, well, when you were shot, you fell and the back of your head struck the side of a rock. This damaged your occipital lobe."

"I-Is it temporary?"

"We performed surgery and found extensive damage and swelling in the brain, Major. However, surgery went very well. We will know for certain once the swelling subsides. There is a good possibility that you may see one day, but right now it is too soon to tell."

"I-I can't breath," I gasped.

I desperately struggled for oxygen.

"Please take deep breaths, Major Seth. You're hyperventilating."

A vortex of irrationality swept over me. If I could just penetrate the darkness, everything would be all right.

"I need light!"

Trying to tear off the bandages, I clawed at the gauze that covered my eyes,

Dr. Sharma grabbed my arms.

I tried to struggle but felt increasingly light-headed and fatigued.

"No! No!"

"Major Seth, please calm down! Nurse, get me some..."

The doctor's words faded into blurred noise. Like a warm blanket, unconsciousness embraced me.

*   *   *   *   *

When I awoke, I knew someone was near me. His cologne was so strong I felt queasy. His breathing sounded as loud as a decrepit asthmatic suffering from pneumonia.

A scrape from a chair, the drip of the intravenous, someone sighing in the distance all seemed unbearably loud. The faint scent of urine and disinfectant now burned my nostrils. I shivered from the draft coming from the overhead fan.

With the loss of my sight, all of my other senses had heightened. I found it unnerving.

I turned my head towards the stranger.

"Who are you?" I asked.

"General Sanjay Singh, Major Seth."

"What do you want?"

"We need you to debrief us. I've been specifically requested by New Delhi to take control of this investigation due to the gravity of the situation."

"Islam Ahmed?"

"Yes. Killed himself before we got him. Cyanide tooth."

I did not say a word, trying to sort out the waves of emotions that crashed through me.

"The Enemy is contending that we kidnapped one of its citizens and falsified evidence of his death on our side of the Line of Control. Tensions are high and we need your assistance before this explodes into a major conflict. Major Seth, are you following me?"

"Yes," I said, not caring.

"We still have several questions that we must have

answered. What happened within that cabin before we arrived? Only you can fill in the gaps in our intelligence, which are vital for national interests."

"Later," I said.

I wanted to sleep and never wake up.

"But..." The General sighed. "Very well. We can speak at another time...Major, my sincerest condolences on the tragic loss of your brother. He will be cremated as a brave hero of India."

A hero of India. You got your wish, brother.

I turned my back to the General signaling the conversation was over. After some time, I heard him stand to his feet.

"General Singh?"

"Yes?"

"Where am I?"

"A military hospital outside New Delhi. You were airlifted here from Kashmir three days ago. You should be thankful to be alive, Major. A soldier was killed saving your life."

I did not respond, envying the dead soldier.

*   *   *   *   *

Over the next weeks my mornings were spent debriefing General Singh. My afternoons were spent in rehabilitation, learning to walk and adjust to my visual handicap.

The days went by quickly, and I grew to enjoy speaking to General Singh. He sympathized with my ordeal and became more of a mentor and a therapist rather than my superior officer.

Doctor Sharma was also a very likeable man, filled with humor. With the doctor's assistance I learned to walk without even the slightest limp.

I was a dutiful patient in every respect except for the gauzes that covered my head. The perpetual itching drove me crazy. I often dug my fingernails into my hand until I drew blood to prevent myself from tearing them off.

Realizing my discomfort, Doctor Sharma reminded me how imperative the bandages were. They were essential to give my eyes time to heal properly and the swelling in my brain to subside from the surgery. He felt encouraged by how quickly I had recovered from my other injuries. This was a very good sign, he often said. I was grateful for his positive demeanor, and successfully resisted my temptation to be liberated from my mask of gauze.

As my days were full of activity and hope, my nights were restless and filled with despair.

The time when the hospital ward shut down for the night and I tried to fall asleep was unbearable. There was nothing to distract me, to escape the past, and the burden of guilt became my penance.

During those endless nights, I wallowed in anguish and prayed for sleep.

I had sworn to protect Inder, and instead he had protected me with his brave demise. I had betrayed my own blood. Because of my weakness my sister-in-law was a widow, her child fatherless.

I replayed that fateful night. I considered countless scenarios to save my brother from being beaten or killed. I could have tried to stop them, but didn't.

Why? Why had I just stood there and done nothing while they beat him so brutally? When Islam had handed me the revolver, why hadn't I used it on them? Aziz was unarmed, massaging his knuckles at that time. I didn't know the revolver was unloaded. The opportunity was perfect to seize.

141

Why had I not reacted?

Excuses filled me.

Everything happened too fast. I was overwhelmed by the truth of my brother's infidelity. I instinctively knew the revolver was empty. I was outnumbered three-to-one. The opportune moment never came.

Inevitably, I could not deny the truth.

My pain and remorse stemmed from my *own* weakness and had nothing to do with losing my sibling. I had thrown up that night not because my brother had been shot, but because I was afraid. Sheer, raw, and absolute terror had crippled me. All I had cared about was saving myself. All I had yearned for was to run away. My terror was so consuming that I had not given a damn for my brother's death. My own survival was all that mattered. I had done nothing because I hadn't cared what happened to Inder.

The awareness of my utter cowardice was devastating.

Sleep provided no solace. When I eventually fell into a fitful slumber, I would suffer the same recurring nightmare—of the one-eyed monster, Cyclopes. I was strung up from the ceiling of the cabin. The wooden walls echoed Islam's chilling laugh and my screams as he repeatedly tortured me. Even in his death, I could not escape his torment.

The nightmares forced me to confront my deepest fears.

I realized that despite knowing the truth about myself, I *still* would not hesitate killing my brother again if given the opportunity to save myself. I *still* did not care that he was dead. If forced, I *still* would raise the revolver and pull the trigger.

My agony was for my own shortcomings as a man and a soldier, and had nothing to do with the loss of my brother.

Now that I was blind, I clearly saw who I was. I may have saved myself from death, but I had condemned my soul. Was this the price of war? Was sacrificing my brother and my honor worth such a cost?

I abhorred myself. I was beyond redemption. I wanted my miserable existence to end, yet lacked the courage to do so.

I realized that I deserved to be blind. I deserved to suffer as a frightened cripple lost in eternal darkness. To always be afraid and perpetually drown in my own fear was fitting retribution.

Death, and the eternal peace it promised, was too merciful a punishment.

*   *   *   *   *

"Are you ready?" Doctor Sharma asked.

"Oh yes, I've been waiting a month for these cursed rags to be taken off my head," I said. "And I long for a proper bath."

"Hold still, then."

"Hello, Amar," said a friendly voice.

"Oh, General, I'm so pleased you found time for my unmasking!" I said.

The doctor began to unwrap the tightly wound gauze around my head.

I was eternally grateful to General Singh. Through much patience and kindness, he had made me confront my nearly debilitating remorse, and understand that what had transpired that night was not my fault. No soldier would have reacted differently in my circumstances, especially after witnessing their brother's death. He had made me realize that my brave actions and quick thinking had led to the demise of my brother's murderers and brought justice to his memory.

The General also made me see that Inder had valiantly helped save the lives of countless Indians by drawing out Islam Ahmed from hiding. My brother was a true, recognized hero of India, as he had always wanted to be. His death had not been in vain.

General Singh had helped me grieve for my brother and brought peace to my soul. He taught me that in God's merciful eyes every soul could be rescued, including mine. Thanks to General Singh, I had decided to dedicate my life in helping those soldiers who had suffered like me. General Singh had become a lifelong friend.

"I wouldn't miss this for the world, Amar," the General said warmly. "Are you looking forward to seeing your family?"

"Yes, thanks to your encouragement and support, I'm ready to meet them. Especially my brother's wife, Nandani. I made a promise to my dear brother that I must keep."

"If you keep talking, I'll never get these things off," the doctor complained.

Sanjay and I fell silent as the doctor gently performed his duties.

When he was finished, the doctor gently said: "Okay, Amar, slowly open your eyes."

I tentatively opened my eyes, and winced with pain from the light. Shards of pain stabbed my skull. I squeezed my eyes shut.

"Turn off the lights," General Singh ordered. "Try now, Amar."

I slowly opened my eyes and blinked furiously, allowing my eyes to adjust.

There was enough natural light coming through the edges of the blinds and underneath a door to make out fuzzy shapes.

I gasped as the shapes began to clear and focus.

"I can see! My God, it's a miracle!" I cried joyously, pressing the doctor's hand.

I noticed the doctor's grim face.

"Doctor, why aren't you smiling?" I asked.

The doctor did not respond. He stepped back and avoided my quizzical look.

I became aware that I was in a small concrete room. The silhouette of a man stood near the window.

"What's going on here, General?" I asked anxiously. "What type of hospital is this?"

There was no reply.

I stood up and approached the General.

The blinds were raised.

I screamed.

The one-eyed man, the devil from my nightmares, appeared from the shadows. He was dressed in a General's uniform.

"No, it can't be! Islam is *dead!*"

"You mean, General Sanjay Singh, don't you?" he mocked, perfectly mimicking the man that everyday for the past month had lent his shoulder for me to cry on, and given me the strength to endure the loss of my brother.

"No, Amar, my *friend,* unlike your brother that you cowardly betrayed, I'm very much alive," he said.

His lips pressed into a cruel smile as he turned off a tape recorder.

Silence replaced the familiar background noise of the hospital.

"*Who* are you?" I cried.

Two guards stood behind the one-eyed monster, their handguns drawn.

"Anonymity has its advantages in my business," he said in Urdu, switching to the accent he had used at the cabin and brothel.

I bolted towards the door, the delicate pieces of my world crashing.

"Let him be," the General chuckled coldly. "He's given us enough intelligence to be a permanent thorn in Kashmir."

I stumbled through the door and screamed out with alarm.

On my knees in defeated tears, I stared with horror at the white crescent moon emblazoned on the green and white flag that fluttered over the military compound.

Mark Gillerstein

"Courage is not the lack of fear.
It is acting in spite of it."

Mark Twain

I was the first boy to run into the change room. My shirt was already half off as I stopped in front of the bench furthest from the showers. I was determined to change as quickly as possible, afraid of what might transpire in a few moments if I did not move faster.

As I took off my shorts, I kept my back to the growing activity around me. I was embarrassed to show my frail, bony frame to the other thirteen-year olds.

I turned wide-eyed as Spud McKenzie burst into the bustling change room. There was a smirk on his sweaty face and a devilish glint in his eyes. His two muscular cronies followed, their faces equally menacing.

My heart pounded against my scrawny chest.

I quickened my pace. I turned towards the brick wall and wished myself to be invisible as I fumbled to put my jeans on.

"Hey, Pussy?"

I whirled around in terror as Spud McKenzie towered over me.

"It's Pushee, Spud. My name is Alvin Pushee," I said uneasily.

Spud's eyes narrowed as he leaned forward. His breath reeked of dead fish.

"That's what I said—*Pussy*."

His two cronies chuckled.

"Hey, Pussy?" he repeated with a growl.

I didn't know what to say. I felt like Spud was a

149

killer Doberman, sensing my fear and ready to pounce.

I reached for my T-shirt and hoped he would leave me alone.

"Answer me when I talk to you!" he barked.

Spud snatched my shirt from my shaking hands and threw it on the ground.

"Hey, Pussy?"

I remained frozen, not saying a word. I was certain any move or response would further provoke him. I prayed he would grow bored of me and find another target.

"Hey, *Pussy?*"

"Y-Yes, Spud?"

"Purple nurple!"

He grabbed my nipples and twisted them harshly, as if he was trying to rip them off.

I hollered with pain and fell to my knees. I covered my throbbing nipples with my hands.

Spud and his goons shrieked with laughter and gave each other high-fives.

"Hey, Pussy?" he said again.

I stared at the floor, determined not to let him enjoy my tears. I noticed my crumpled shirt on the yellowing concrete and shivered in the cold. I wrapped my arms around myself.

"Are you deaf, Pussy?" Spud demanded.

I noticed that the rowdiness of the change room was gone. It was absolutely silent. Every boy's eyes were on us.

"Hey, Pussy?"

He slapped me across the top of my head.

With envy, I watched as an ant scurried past Spud's feet and disappeared safely into a crack in the concrete.

"Answer me, you fuckin' *Nigger!*"

Spud grabbed a handful of my sweaty hair and pulled me to my feet, ignoring my cries of pain and help.

"That's enough, Spud. Let him go."

I wept with relief as Mark Gillerstein moved towards us, his face flushed with resolve.

Mark Gillerstein was neither a friend nor a foe of mine. He was a quiet and respected member of the class, known for his good heart and composed demeanor.

Spud let go of me, enraged at the disruption.

Pressing my back against the wall, I cowered in the corner. My hands covered my swollen nipples. Tears streamed down my face.

"*What* did you say?" Spud sneered, looking down at Mark.

"He's done nothing to you. Let him be," Mark said.

Mark stepped in front of me.

"Get out of my way, Gillerstein. Or we'll make you."

"No."

A pronounced vein on Spud's head pulsed with fury.

"I said, *move!*"

Lips pressed firmly with resolve, Mark defiantly stood his ground.

Spud laughed as his friends encircled Mark.

"Do you have a death wish, Gillerstein? I'm warning you."

"No, Spud, I'm warning *you.*"

Someone snickered.

Spud glared at the boys in the change room.

"No one tells me what to do. *No one!*" he screamed,

and lunged at Mark.

With remarkable speed Mark ducked underneath the swinging fist and made contact with Spud's jaw with a vicious uppercut.

Spud's teeth slammed together and his eyes rolled into the back of his head.

The bully that had terrorized me for months collapsed in front of me—motionless.

I watched in petrified silence as Mark took on both of Spud's friends.

None of the other students came to Mark's aid. Everyone watched in silent horror. The sound of fists striking flesh and my own whimpering filled the change room.

I do not know when Mr. Davidson, our gym teacher, rushed into the change room and broke up the fight. Time had lost all meaning. The next thing I knew, the change room was empty.

Mr. Davidson handed me my dirt-stained T-shirt and told me to get dressed.

*   *   *   *   *

I numbly mouthed the lyrics to *The Sound of Music* that the class sung, my eyes focused on the light reflecting off Mr. Rosewood's bald spot.

After I had changed, Mr. Davidson had taken me to speak with the Principal. After recounting what had happened, she had told me to return to my music class, as if nothing had occurred. I wanted to ask what had happened to Spud and Mark, but instead complied without a word.

"Very, very good," Mr. Rosewood said, his thin moustache quivering with pleasure. "Sopranos, make sure you sing together and maintain the high notes."

The door to the classroom opened and Mark Gillerstein walked in. His left eye was swollen shut, a ghastly shade of dark purple.

"Ah, Mark, my Tenor, come in, come in." Mr. Rosewood chirped. "We are singing 'Do-Re-Mi.'"

Mr. Rosewood beamed as Mark sat down and opened his songbook.

"Okay, class, from the top."

As the class sang, I stared at Mark. I marveled at his valor and was overwhelmed with gratitude. I had never done anything to warrant his help, but he had saved me—fearlessly.

I yearned to have an iota of the courage that Mark possessed.

Then, as if in slow motion, I watched incredulously as one tear slowly accumulated in Mark's good eye and rolled down his bruised face.

No, it can't be. Is it possible? I wondered, stunned. *Had he been afraid? Is he still afraid?*

I noticed that Mark's songbook was shaking in his hands.

I was thunderstruck by the truth.

Mark was just as scared as I was, but still had confronted Spud *despite* his fears.

A lump grew in my throat and sorrow filled my heart.

Mark's courage and bravery were far greater than I had anticipated. He had acted not because he was fearless, but because it was the right thing to do.

Yet if he felt the same way I had then...

Why didn't I stand up to Spud?

Mark had conquered his fears by acting courageously while I had cowered, impotent and pathetic.

Is that what I am? A coward?

No, I thought, refusing to accept such a terrible

possibility. *If Mark can feel fear like me, then I can become brave like him.*

As Rodgers and Hammerstein's inspiring music resounded throughout the room, I vowed that I would do everything in my power to become like Mark Gillerstein.

*　　　*　　　*　　　*　　　*

The bully's name in high school was ironically Julius Hunter. He preyed on immigrants. Unlike Spud McKenzie, who was tall and muscular and a natural athlete, Julius was thick and short, like a thug for the mafia. Despite being under five-and-a-half feet tall, Julius's viciousness and cleverness were copious. No one dared to stop his cruelty on the immigrants.

I had managed to go through the first half of Grade 9 invisible to Julius Hunter, or for that matter by any other student in my new school. I had mastered the art of blending into the background—of not drawing attention to myself. I was so quiet and generic in my manners and actions that even my teachers had trouble remembering who I was.

I was a shadow, clandestinely observing the world passing around me, and very content to live such an existence.

In their T-shirts and shorts, the students waited for the arrival of Ms. Blackthorn, our gym teacher— she was always boasting how she was more of a man than any of us, especially when she would pummel us during dodge ball.

Today was the final day for basketball. Each student had taken a basketball from the caged, wheeled container that was in the center of the gymnasium.

Standing obscurely in one corner of the gym, I

154

dribbled my basketball and scrutinized Julius Hunter. I wondered when Ms. Blackthorn would show up to begin the lesson.

After five minutes of miserably trying to dunk the ball, Julius turned his attention to what he was much better at—tormenting foreigners.

For days Julius had been harassing these newly immigrated twins from China. He called them 'Dim Bums'—an expression I thought wasn't very clever for someone as smart as Julius. With their limited understanding of English, the twins thought he was mispronouncing the Chinese delicacy rather than making fun of them.

So far Julius had only bullied the twins verbally, but I knew he was becoming restless. He was primed to provoke the twins further.

I was surprised when Julius ignored the twins. His attention seemed to be focused on Harinder Jagdev, a bloated Sikh boy who had transferred to our school earlier that day.

I watched as Julius motioned his own henchman over and whispered to them. I knew by his malicious expression that things were about to become very bad for Harinder.

Julius and his three friends crossed the gymnasium and surrounded Harinder.

The ball was knocked from Harinder's hands. He screamed for help as the bullies grabbed him and tore off his T-shirt.

The ruckus of bouncing balls and conversation throughout the gymnasium ceased.

Where was Ms. Blackthorn? I thought anxiously. I hoped she would come soon before things got worse.

Julius and his goons lifted Harinder by his arms and legs and dropped him into the empty basketball cage. The cage door—which opened from the top—was closed over Harinder.

Julius slid the cage's latch into the locking position.

The other students surrounded the cage.

I moved closer as Julius spun the cage in circles.

Inside the cage, his fingers wrapped around the steel mesh to steady himself, Harinder pleaded to be left alone.

This was a form of terrorizing that I had never witnessed before. Although I sympathized for what Harinder was experiencing, I was grateful it was him in the cage instead of me.

Thrilled by the attention he was receiving, Julius stopped spinning the cage and said: "Look at his hairy back! He's a hairy, stinking monkey. Harry the Monkey, a worthless animal who belongs in a cage!"

Everyone laughed, including the Oriental twins, who didn't even understand what Julius was saying.

Harinder's acne-strewn face was filled with terror as Julius and his friends poked and prodded him through the cage.

I froze as Harinder's desperate eyes found mine.

"Help me, please!" he cried.

Suddenly the image of Mark Gillerstein's noble face filled my mind. I knew he would not have hesitated to stop such madness, such cruelty.

But I remained immobilized, shaking inside with fear. And then the ugly truth dawned upon me: I was incapable of ever being like Mark Gillerstein.

I *was* a coward.

Instead of heroically helping Harinder, I pretended to laugh, pointing at him like the other students.

I was horrified and repulsed by my behavior. I was worse than any of my classmates because I knew exactly what kind of pain and humiliation I was causing Harinder.

Thankfully, Ms. Blackthorn entered the gymnasium and freed Harinder. As she reprimanded Julius and his remorseless accomplices, I rushed into the bathroom and threw up.

*   *   *   *   *

After the incident with the basketball cage, Harinder suffered other humiliations during the month, from being stripped and tied to the showerhead in the change room to receiving wedgies in the cafeteria in front of half the school.

The following month, Harinder didn't show up for English or Physical Education, the two classes we had together.

I lost my ability to eat or sleep, plagued by the consequences of my inaction. I imagined the worst scenarios—Harinder had slit his wrists or jumped onto a freeway or emptied a bottle of Aspirin down his throat.

Then, at lunch one Friday, I overheard Julius planning his greatest prank—to kidnap Harinder once he emerged from hiding, and reunite him with his brothers and sisters in the chimpanzee enclosure at the zoo.

At the end of last period that day, I apprehensively approached my English teacher, Mrs. Marshall. This was no small feat as Mrs. Marshall intimidated the heck out of me. Her long neck, sharp teeth, curved fingernails, and bird-like face resembled a Velociraptor.

"E-Excuse me, Mrs. Marshall?"

She turned from the chalkboard she was erasing.

Her face scrunched up as she tried to remember my name.

"Yes...?"

"Alvin, Mrs. Marshall. Alvin Pushee."

"Of course. Yes, Alvin, what can I do for you?"

"Um, I was wondering if you knew what happened to Harinder Jagdev?"

"Oh yes, the new student. Most unfortunate."

I paled. A surge of dizziness swept through me.

What had been Harinder's demise? Strangulation? Electrocution? No, probably a slit artery or a fifty-floor dive onto rush hour traffic. That's what I would have done.

"W-What happened?" I managed to croak.

"I am not at liberty to discuss his condition."

"Please, Mrs. Marshall. I'm a close friend and haven't been able to get in touch with him. I'm concerned."

I was impressed at the uncharacteristic conviction I told my lie with.

She studied me for a long time and I wondered whether she had seen through my deception.

"Very well. If that's the case, I don't see the harm in you knowing," she said.

She cleared her throat and adjusted her bifocals.

"Unfortunately, Harinder's body has rejected his recently transplanted kidney. He is very, very sick. I believe he's at Memorial Hospital."

*　　　*　　　*　　　*　　　*

I queasily entered the hospital room. All the machines, tubes, wires and needles connected to Harinder were unnerving.

I tried not to look at the intravenous pumping into

Harinder's veins or the urine flowing from the catheter that snaked out from beneath the blanket.

If there was one thing that scared me more than being bullied at school, it was needles, blood, operations, or pretty much anything that had to do with hospitals.

Harinder's eyes fluttered open. He looked at me, his gaze hazy. Then, much to my surprise, his eyes suddenly cleared and widened with recognition.

"My name is Alvin Pushee," I said nervously.

"What do *you* want?" he asked. "Are you here to laugh at me? Do you want to mock me like your friends?"

My friends?

I shuddered at the thought of being a friend of Julius Hunter or Spud McKenzie, but painfully understood why Harinder had made such an accusation.

"I-I'm very sorry about that. What I did was...was inexcusable. I hate, really *hate* myself for it. I can understand why you'd be angry with me."

Harinder seemed shocked by my apology.

His eyes narrowed.

"Is this a *joke*?"

"No, Harinder. That's why I'm here. To apologize."

"Why?"

"Why?" I repeated stupidly.

"Yeah, *why*? Are you family?"

"Uh...no."

"A friend?"

"Um...not exactly."

"Then why would you want to apologize to someone like *me*?"

I knew he was referring to his scarred, puffy face

159

and hairy body.

I avoided the painful look in his eyes, shocked at how much he despised himself.

Harinder turned from me and looked out the window.

It was a beautiful, sunny day, one of those days when the entire population seemed to go outside and momentarily capture and embrace the joys of life.

"Do you know what the purpose of the kidneys are?" Harinder asked quietly.

"No."

"The purpose of the kidney is to maintain a proper electrolyte and water balance. It regulates the acid-base concentration and filters the blood of metabolic wastes, which are excreted as urine," Harinder intoned, as if he was reading from a medical dictionary.

I was silent, not sure what to say.

"Ironic, isn't it?" Harinder laughed hollowly. "My own body is unable to remove the waste within me. As if *it* believes my purpose is to accumulate waste, not dispose of it. Like I am a genetically programmed garbage can. They're right what they say at school, that I'm a 'worthless animal.' God, I *do* belong in a cage."

"No, Harinder, that's not true."

"Are you fuckin' crazy? *Look at me!*"

Harinder covered his face as he burst into tears.

I sat on the edge of the bed, careful not to sit on any of the multitude of wires and tubes.

After a moment of uncertainty, I put my hand on Harinder's shaking shoulder.

"No, get away from me!" he shouted, flinching from my touch.

I pulled my hand back, shaken by his outburst.

A photograph of a young, smiling Harinder sat on the bedside table. It was before his kidneys had begun to fail, when he was thirteen-years old. He was standing by the edge of a swimming pool, his body hairless and defined. His face was acne free and without a trace of fat. It was a handsome face, a happy face.

I remembered Harinder's mother telling me earlier that day that her son was an exceptional swimmer before he became sick. I was shocked at the side effects of the anti-rejection medicines he had taken after his first transplant. The transformation of his face and body in only a year was staggering.

"Harinder, have you ever seen the movie, *Teenwolf*?"

Harinder's sobbing diminished. He still covered his face, but I knew he was listening, curious at my unusual question.

"In the movie, Michael J. Fox is half teenager and half wolf. At first he's terrified that he looks different. But the great thing is that he becomes the coolest kid at school, despite the way he looks."

What the heck am I doing talking about Teenwolf? I wondered.

"Yeah, but he was an *amazing* basketball player. That's why he was cool. His wolf-like powers made him so," Harinder said, meeting my eyes.

I thought about that for a minute, and then shook my head.

"That's not true. In the final game he doesn't use his wolf-like powers and *still* wins the championship by inspiring his team. You see, he was cool through confidence and perseverance."

I winced inside at how stupid I sounded.

Then the most amazing thing happened.

Harinder smiled, and that beautiful person in the photograph was suddenly sitting in front of me.

161

*   *   *   *   *

"My dear friends and family, thank you all for coming to our wedding. Meena and I are delighted and honored that you could share this celebration with us."

The opulent banquet hall echoed from the round of applause. Some people tapped their wine glasses with their forks, urging the newly married couple to kiss.

"There will be many moments to shower my lovely bride with affection once I finish what I have to say."

The banquet hall grew silent.

"Thank you. There are *so* many people I have to thank for everything they've done for me, for their patience and love and time. I am very blessed. But, before I do, there is one person in particular that I am forever indebted to. The one person who saved me at my most dire moment. My best man and best friend, Alvin Pushee."

Sitting at the head table, my heart froze.

Harinder and Meena looked at me from the podium and smiled.

"Many of you know that ten years ago I was very sick," Harinder continued. "Both my kidneys had failed when I was thirteen and I had to get a new kidney. To prevent my immune system from attacking my new kidney I had to take immuno-suppressants. These drugs minimize the chance of my body rejecting the new kidney. What many of you *don't* know, however, is that I stopped taking those drugs."

A murmur of surprise filled the banquet hall.

"I was unable to bear the drugs' side effects—tremendous body and facial hair, weight gain and brutal acne. Just *one* of these side effects would be a nightmare for any teenager—case in point, my younger sister, Preeti, who recently had an indiscernible pimple on her forehead and locked herself in her room for two days!"

The crowd chuckled.

Harinder smiled warmly at his sister, who blushed with embarrassment.

"As I was saying, I had *all* these terrible side effects in abundance. I wanted nothing more than just to be a normal kid, not a freak show that was constantly tormented and humiliated at school. I had lost all my friends once I became ill and *no one* at my high school could even bear looking at me. I even transferred to a new school, but things only became worse. So, I gave up. And, as a result of my failure to keep up with my medications, my new kidney slowly failed."

Harinder's face was filled with pain as he recollected the past.

"To my parent's horror I told them that I had no desire to get another transplant. I also refused to be treated indefinitely with machines to remove the waste from my body. I had chosen death over being an unwanted freak."

I was shocked. I had no idea how close Harinder had come to death.

"My parents spent countless hours pleading, crying, and trying guilt me to change my mind. But I just wanted the pain to end. I was inconsolable, filled with rage and bitterness. There was even a match for another new kidney—something that can take years to find—but I declined to have it, much to my parents despair. The kidney was given to another recipient."

Harinder paused. Meena affectionately squeezed his hand, encouraging him to continue.

"Eventually, my parents realized that if I had no will to live, then there was nothing they could do. They resigned to the fact that they would soon lose their only son."

The stunned silence in the banquet hall was deafening. Every person was engrossed by Harinder's story.

"Then, a miracle happened. Alvin Pushee entered our lives. He approached my parents, and offered his assistance. My parents were delighted, assuming he was a new friend I had made at school. But, he wasn't. Alvin told them that he was a stranger who wanted to offer *his* kidney."

I unconsciously fingered my scar through my dress shirt as Harinder spoke.

"I mean *who* does that, right? My parents thought he was mad. But, they got him tested once they confirmed with his parents that he had permission and was serious. And what did Alvin do when he was getting his blood taken from him? He broke into a sweat, pale as a ghost, and fainted. My parents couldn't understand it. Why was a strange boy, who didn't even know their son, willing to donate his kidney when he couldn't even handle the sight of a syringe?"

I glanced at Harry's parents, who smiled tenderly at me. Their eyes sparkled with tears.

"Amazingly, Alvin had the same blood type and tissue type—virtually a perfect match. It was as if he was *always* a member of my family, *always* my brother!"

Meena—looking stunning in her saffron silk sari—mouthed the word 'thank you' to me.

I smiled at the woman I had grown to love as my sister.

"But, that was *not* the miracle, my friends," Harinder enthused. "No, the miracle was the other lifelong gifts Alvin gave me. He gave me friendship when no one else would. He taught me how to skate and ski, and I trained his taste buds to the intricacies of Indian food. He taught me the beauty of camping and I taught him how to Bhangra dance. And I'm a damn good teacher because that man now dances Bhangra like he has Punjabi fire in his blood."

Harinder's expression became serious once the laughter subsided.

"Alvin also taught me that kindness, compassion, love, and perseverance conquers any side-effects. Without his motivation, I would have likely rejected his kidney as well. Alvin not only saved my life that day he stepped into my hospital room, but he also made me appreciate life every day thereafter."

Harinder turned, speaking directly to me.

"And most important, Alvin, my dear, dear, friend and brother that I never had, you showed me what true courage is. And for that gift I cannot ever repay you."

I looked down at my trembling hands.

Is it possible? I wondered, the thought never crossing my mind before. *Can it be true?*

Harinder and Meena lifted their glasses. Their faces were filled with gratitude and love.

"Would everyone please raise your glasses?"

I watched dumbfounded as three hundred people stood and saluted their glasses at me.

"To Alvin Pushee. The bravest man I know."

"To Alvin!" they all declared in unison.

Everyone looked at me the way I had once looked at a thirteen-year old boy with a swollen eye in music class.

My whole body shuddered as I wept.

I had done it.

I was Mark Gillerstein.

Faith
&
Hope

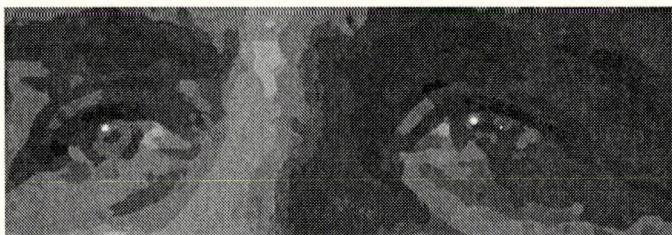

The Man of Faith

"When faith is lost, when honor dies,
the man is dead."

John Greenleaf Whittier

General Jacek Kania limped through the quiet snowy streets of Poznan. A white dust descended from the dark overcast sky as he crossed the bridge overlooking the ice-encrusted Warta River. The only sound emanated from his boots crunching against the hard snow.

Despite the merciless cold, the General loved walking the empty streets in the midst of night. He never felt more alive than when the bitter cold penetrated his layers, as if the very marrow within his bones were freezing. The icy bite of the Polish winter invigorated him, reminding him of his childhood.

Kania approached two guards from the Russian controlled Polish Army, who were smoking to keep warm beside a heavily armored T-54 tank.

The soldiers tossed their cigarettes aside and snapped to fearful attention at the sight of the General.

Kania's rise to power within the Red Army was legendary, and was based less on his brilliant military tactics than on his unwavering loyalty and ruthlessness. According to rumor, Stalin had especially favored Kania. In fact, he was nicknamed by his soldiers 'The Tyrant,' a name that suited the unmarried, childless General well.

The chiseled lines in his weathered face hardened as the General walked past the petrified men. He noticed the soldiers eyeing his artificial leg.

As he did every night, Kania limped into the

square in the center of the city and stopped in front of Poznan's city hall.

Amazing how snow can mask all traces of blood, he pondered.

As his mind traveled back in time, the snow melted from the square and a mass of protesting people materialized before him.

It was June 1953, six months earlier. The workers from a large metallurgical factory in Poznan had declared a strike for better pay. Within a day, news of the strike spread across the nation. Demonstrations for change and liberation from Russian control were sparked throughout Poland. Within Poznan, over a hundred thousand anti-government protestors congregated towards city hall. Many were armed and their anger mounted with each step.

Being a Polish-born Russian soldier, General Kania had been specifically selected by his superiors in Moscow. His orders were to crush the Polish anti-communist movement. The Kremlin felt that sending a loyal Pole to persecute and kill other Poles was a particularly powerful political statement.

They had been right.

Staring impassively at the chanting mob from the turret of his tank, General Kania had acted without hesitation and ordered his troops to open fire upon his own countrymen.

The General blinked and gasped as the memory before him changed.

Dozens of dead and hundreds of injured suddenly lay before him, their blood collecting in the cracks between the cobblestones.

Footsteps behind the General snapped his reverie.

"Urgh!" Kania cried out as a sharp pain exploded from the back of his skull.

Kania collapsed onto the snowy ground.

He turned, trying to look at the assailant who hurriedly searched his pockets. He only managed to see a hazy silhouette looming over him for a moment before he blacked out.

*   *   *   *   *

"Comrade General?"

Kania groaned.

"Comrade General, are you alright?"

Kania opened his eyes to see the young face of one of his lieutenants glancing down at him with concern. The two smoking soldiers Kania had seen earlier stood nearby, their rifles pointing towards the threatening shadows that lurked around the periphery of the square.

"Yes, Lieutenant Kamenev, I am."

The General grimaced as he was helped to his feet. He rubbed the back of his throbbing head.

"Were you assaulted, sir?"

"Your keen powers of observation should be commended, Comrade Lieutenant," Kania snapped sarcastically. "Now if I'm not mistaken, isn't this sector of the city under *your* command during the night?"

"Y-Yes, Comrade General," the young officer stammered. "But I have pleaded with you on several occasions to take an armed escort during your walks, especially during this time of night. You should even have guards posted at your home. A Russian General living alone without protection is a great risk. There are dissidents prowling everywhere to assassinate such a political target."

Kania glared at the young man with his piercing ice-blue eyes.

"If you did your job properly, Comrade Lieutenant, then I would not require armed escorts or security at my home, now would I? Issue an order that any citizen caught out past curfew will be shot and detained if he or she unfortunately survives. Is that clear?"

"Perfectly, Comrade General."

"And if you can't provide adequate security, Comrade Lieutenant, I'll have you re-stationed in Siberia, and find someone who can. *Understood?*"

"Yes, Comrade General," the lieutenant said anxiously.

"Now get out of my sight."

"B-But your safety!"

General Kania's glare silenced the subordinate, who reluctantly saluted and signaled his two guards to follow him.

The General waited until the men had disappeared before examining his pockets.

He cursed in his native Polish tongue as he realized his wallet was gone. Although there had been little money in it, several key pieces of identification would have to be replaced. Worse, he had lost a treasured photograph of his beloved father.

The General unbuttoned his coat and checked his vest pocket. He was relieved to find his gold pocket watch, his most prized possession.

Irritated that his nightly stroll had been blemished, the General wearily headed home.

*　　*　　*　　*　　*

"What's the state of Stalingrad?" Josef Vissarionovich Stalin asked, as he slowly loaded his revolver with the six bullets aligned on his gleaming desk.

"The Nazi's have taken approximately eighty-percent of the city and have pushed our forces to the Volga River," General Kania said.

Kania stood stiffly and avoided the fierce gaze from the Dictator of the Soviet Union.

"Go on, Comrade General."

"We've suffered heavy casualties, and with the Italian, Hungarian, and Romanian forces supporting Hitler, our defensive lines are on the verge of collapse."

Stalin loaded the gun without comment.

Holding the revolver, he turned and looked out the large bay window. He surveyed the autumn sun setting behind the Kremlin in silence.

"Comrade General, how long have you known me?" he finally asked, turning to face Kania.

"Sixteen years."

"And when have I *ever* tolerated such inexcusable defeatist words?" Stalin roared, firing all six bullets into the General's leg.

Kania awoke screaming.

Although his left leg no longer existed, he still somehow felt the searing pain from the bullets that Stalin had shot him with.

Trembling from the nightmare that still lingered within his mind, Kania reached for the glass of water by his bedside. He emptied the glass, and wiped the sweat from his face. For a long time he stared dully at his wooden leg, waiting for his heart to calm down.

Stalin is dead and can no longer hurt you, he reminded himself.

The sudden banging at his front door startled Kania.

Muttering, he got out of bed, put on a robe, and limped out of his bedroom.

The banging grew in desperate intensity.

"I'm coming!" he shouted impatiently in Polish.

The General unbolted and swung open the door.

"What is it?"

Kania stepped back warily at the sight of the black-coated stranger, whose gaunt face seemed more pale than the snow that covered him.

"Please, help me," the stranger gasped and collapsed into Kania's arms.

*   *   *   *   *

The General sat by the bed, studying the unconscious man with disbelief. He was certain that this man was the son of Father Prazmowska, the priest of the local parish that Kania had attended as a child. Upon his return to Poznan, Kania had heard from local citizens that Father Prazmowska had been killed during the bombing of the city near the end of World War II, and that his son, Adam Prazmowska, had taken over the parish.

Kania stared at his wallet, an old pipe, and a crumpled paper bag filled with brown-powdered heroin that sat on his lap.

What happened to this man of the cloth?

After laying the young Father Prazmowska in his own bed, and tending to his terrible fever, the General had searched the stranger's frayed trench coat to verify the identity of the man. He was stunned to discover his own stolen wallet and the addictive opiate.

The young priest stirred.

The General pocketed his wallet, and dumped the pipe and heroin into the top drawer of the bedside table.

Father Prazmowska eyes opened, and he gasped with fear.

"Who are you?!"

"I'm the man whose door you nearly broke down last night. Don't you remember?"

"No, I don't. I must leave," the priest said.

Wide-eyed, he anxiously examined his surroundings.

"Lie down, Father Prazmowska. You're not going anywhere. You must eat and allow your body to recover from the fever, which only broke a few hours ago."

"How do you know who I am?" the priest asked.

"I knew your father. Your resemblance to him is uncanny."

"I don't believe you. Where were you born?"

"Here, in Poznan, at the turn of the century, fifty-three years ago."

"You speak excellent Polish, but you have a hint of a Russian accent," the priest observed guardedly.

"Yes, my mother died when I was ten. My father moved my siblings and I to Moscow. I learned Russian there, but recently moved back here, back to my childhood home. Our good family friends watched over this place for all these years. Remarkable that it survived the bombings, isn't it?"

Why am I telling him all of this? Kania wondered. *Why don't I just have this heroin-addicted priest arrested and executed for assaulting me?*

The priest studied the room. He was surprised to see nothing personal—no art or photographs or books. Only items that provided a functional use, such as the wooden chair the strange man sat on and a mirror hanging from the wall, were in the bedroom. It was a cold, empty place.

The priest shivered. He pulled the blanket up to his neck.

"W-What time is it?" he asked, filled with a compulsion to run.

The General extracted a gold pocket watch from his vest that his father had given to him as a gift when he had entered the Red Army. Kania unclasped the lid and studied the Roman numerals.

"Ten past ten in the morning."

The priest stared at the pocket watch.

"I've been here all night? In your bed?"

"I don't require much sleep."

My heavy conscience prevents me from doing so.

The priest leaned back into the pillow, his guard temporarily lowered. He sighed with exhaustion.

"Thank you for helping me...Forgive me, I don't even know the name of the man who so generously gave me his bed."

Kania decided to avoid revealing that he was a General of the Soviet Union.

"Jacek," he said.

"Thank you, Jacek."

"Whom were you running from?"

"Everyone," the priest replied cryptically, his voice distant.

"Do you still preach in the same church as your father did, near the southern end of the city, Father?"

"The church was destroyed during the bombing. And don't call me Father, Jacek."

"May I ask why?"

The priest did not reply. He turned away from the General.

"Father Prazmowska?"

"Damn you, I told you not to call me that! I-I am sorry," he said, aghast at his outburst.

176

The General observed the priest without a word.

"Don't look at me that way, Jacek. I can't stand to be judged. It wasn't my fault. Don't you see? I've not abandoned God. No, God has abandoned *all* of us. I can't give hope to people when I no longer have any faith. No God would allow our people to be ruthlessly humiliated and slaughtered like we were vermin—by first the Germans, then the Russians. For fifteen years I've seen nothing but misery, death, and destruction in this God-forsaken country. My prayers have been to no avail. I've helplessly watched Poles betray other Poles, women raped, and children shot."

Tears welled in the priest's eyes as he spoke with growing agitation.

"I couldn't bear lying to their hopeful faces anymore—trying to assure them that everything would be alright and that God would protect them when things continued to become worse and worse. I felt like clawing my tongue out for the *shit* I uttered*!*" he wailed.

When the crying subsided, the priest continued in a weary whisper.

"I want to run away, Jacek. To escape from the pain and suffering. To forever replace that emptiness in my soul with chemical bliss. I yearn to be oblivious, Jacek. Can you understand that?"

"I think your soup should be ready," Kania said, shaken. "You must eat to regain your strength. I'll be back in a moment."

The General limped out of the room to leave the priest with his despair.

*   *   *   *   *

Kania lay on the couch, emotionally exhausted and unable to sleep. The priest's words repeated in the General's mind.

I've helplessly watched Poles betray other Poles...

Kania squeezed his eyes shut, filled with remorse.

The priest had ranted and cried for several hours, barely touching his soup, his mood swinging from peaks of hyper-anxiety to troughs of depression. His eyes wide, Adam spoke with frenzied urgency, often gripping Kania's hand painfully, as if the General *was* a priest and could provide salvation.

During the entire ordeal, Kania had quietly listened and sympathized with the man's anguish. He wanted to desperately help Adam, believing that saving the man of the cloth would somehow atone for the innumerable sins Kania had committed. Kania knew he was partially to blame for the priest's loss of faith, and he desired nothing more than to restore it to the broken man.

But Kania was also afraid. He was terrified that he would somehow be discovered and charged for treason for assisting a man of God, charged for being an anti-communist.

The General had managed to survive the war *and* Stalin's persecutions that killed millions of Russians by trusting no one. Even after Stalin had shot him, Kania had remained ferociously loyal. He realized any other course of action would cost him his life. He had even avoided marriage and children for fear that those he loved would be used against him, hurt or tortured in some way. He had seen it happen to too many fellow comrades. It was too much of a risk for Kania to bear.

What would my men think if they realized their Comrade General, 'The Tyrant,' was nothing more than a coward?

It was ironic, he thought as sleep enveloped him, that by fearing his life he had avoided living it.

The General turned his thoughts back to the priest. He wondered if he could afford to trust Father Prazmowska. By helping the priest, he drowsily realized that he was taking his own leap of faith, and no one knew better than Kania that no true communist believed in such things.

*   *   *   *   *

Kania awoke to the sound of rustling. He slowly stood up to face the back of the silhouette that was pulling his golden watch from the vest he had hung over the kitchen table.

"Stop, thief!" Kania snarled.

The moon emerged from the clouds.

The General gasped with surprise as the pale light shining through the kitchen window suddenly illuminated the gaunt face.

"Father Prazmowska?"

The priest grabbed the kitchen chair and smashed it against the General.

Kania cried out with pain as oak struck flesh.

He collapsed onto the wooden floor.

"*Why?*" Kania demanded, stung by betrayal.

Father Prazmowska threw the remains of the chair aside and picked up another chair.

He lifted the chair over his head.

The General noted that the priest's eyes seemed devoid of emotion, hollow and blank.

"*Answer me!*" Kania cried as he lifted his arms to defend himself.

With a devilish smile, the priest swung the chair downwards.

*   *   *   *   *

The General regained consciousness to the sound of the open front door banging against its frame from the howling winter wind.

Kania painfully got to his feet. He shut the front door, and stumbled into the bathroom. He grimaced as he gingerly touched the bruise on his forehead, and was thankful that he was not cut. As he washed his face, the telephone rang.

"This is General Kania," he answered with as much authority as he could muster.

"Comrade General, this is Lieutenant Kamanev. Forgive the intrusion, but please come to headquarters immediately."

"What is it?"

"It is a matter of importance, Comrade General. I would prefer not to discuss it over the phone."

"I'll be right there."

Hanging up the phone, Kania limped into the bedroom. He opened his closet, and laboriously dressed into his uniform.

As Kania inspected himself in the bedroom mirror, he noticed in the reflection that the top drawer of the bedside table was ajar. He turned around, and peered inside the drawer.

The heroin and pipe were missing. An empty heroin bag lay beside the bed. Ashes were strewn across the floor

"Blyat!" Kania shouted with rage.

He smashed the bedroom mirror with his fist.

Fists clenched, the General cursed himself for his stupidity.

In the bathroom, Kania picked the glass fragments out of his knuckles and wrapped his bloodied hand with gauze.

Still heaving with anger, the General stormed out of his home.

*　　　*　　　*　　　*　　　*

"Why am I here?" Kania asked Lieutenant Kamanev as they walked through the dreary, underground concrete hallway.

"We caught a man violating the curfew, Comrade General."

"I told you to shoot violators, not to disturb me in the middle of the *bloody* night every time you arrested one," Kania growled.

"This concerns you directly, Comrade General."

The lieutenant opened the metal door to the interrogation room at the end of the hallway.

The General limped into the concrete room. He stared coldly at the bound and bruised Father Prazmowska.

The priest's face was badly battered, his right eye grotesquely swollen shut. Blood poured from a bullet wound in the thigh of the priest's left leg.

The priest's good eye widened with panic as he realized that he had assaulted and stolen from a General of the Red Army.

"What's happening here?" Kania demanded, turning to the lieutenant.

Lieutenant Kamanev pulled out a golden watch from his pocket and dangled it in front of the General.

"Comrade General, we captured this thief with this pocket watch. You name is inscribed in it," he said.

"I see," said the General.

"Is it yours?"

"Yes."

The young lieutenant smiled, imagining his imminent promotion.

"And do you recognize this man, Comrade General?" he asked.

"Of course."

The priest moaned with trepidation.

"He's a guest at my home, and this watch was a gift I gave to him," Kania said.

The color from the lieutenant's face drained.

"E-Excuse me? Comrade General, we found him on the street, running from us."

"Yes, he unfortunately has frequent episodes of sleepwalking. It's quite a problem. I awoke at night and found him missing."

"B-But—"

"Do you dare question *me?*" the General roared. "You've already done enough damage. How dare you treat him in such a manner without first consulting me? I'll have your head on a platter for this outrage!"

"N-No, Comrade General, please. My most humble apologies," the lieutenant said desperately. "I had no idea. He had no identification on him."

"Get out! All of you!"

Lieutenant Kamanev signaled the guards out of the room. He eyed his superior's bruised face and bandaged hand skeptically before quickly shutting the door behind him.

Stone-faced, the General unbuttoned the top button of his uniform and removed a butterfly knife from his pocket.

He stepped towards the prisoner.

"I know who you are!" the priest cried, his face plastered with fear and panic.

A pool of urine formed by the priest's feet.

"You're General Kania, the Tyrant. I didn't know— I'm sorry! Please don't hurt me. I needed the money to get something to make the pain go away. Oh God, I just wanted the pain to go away."

With a flick of the wrist, the General opened the knife and cut the rope tied around the priest's wrists.

Kania put the knife away with a benevolent smile.

Tears of surprise and relief dripped from the priest's good eye.

"Why?" he asked.

The General leaned over until he was inches from the priest's face.

"Faith, Father," he whispered compassionately.

Kania extracted from underneath his uniform a cross made from the very bullets Stalin had shot him with.

"Faith."

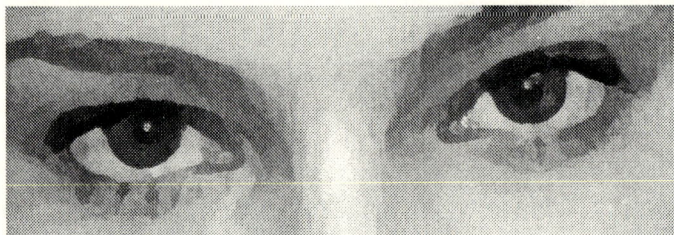

Angel

"A mother's love is instinctual, unconditional, and forever."

Anonymous

Fiona returned her daughter's toothless grin; the baby was enthusiastically playing in the sandbox, streams of sand pouring through her clenched fists.

It was a gorgeous day—the time of year when the rustling leaves began to morph into the colors of autumn and traces of summer could still be felt during the sun's zenith. The sweet melody of children's laughter sang through the hectic neighborhood park, and the arms of the surrounding maples danced in the warm breeze.

The baby eventually lost interest in the sand. She crawled to the periphery of the sandbox, where her mother was sitting on a bench, and raised her arms to signal that she wanted to be lifted.

Must be time for another diaper change, Fiona thought.

Fiona lifted the baby and laid her on the bench. She removed the diaper—still dry. She glanced at her daughter, who intently stared back at her.

Concentration filled the tiny face. The baby opened her mouth as if struggling to speak.

Fiona's heart skipped a beat.

Was this the moment she had yearned for all year? Was her baby going to utter her first word? She had listened to many mothers talk about their baby's first word, and now her moment to share that priceless milestone had finally arrived.

Fiona wondered what her baby's voice would sound like. Would her baby's voice mature and eventually belong to a brilliant lawyer who would enrapture a jury with captivating closing statements? Would it eventually belong to a world famous cardiologist who would shout crisp, confident orders to her team of physicians and nurses while working to save a prominent patient? Fiona suddenly envisioned the voice belonging to a young mother who would fondly read bedtime stories to her children each night, her gentle and loving voice lulling them into a peaceful slumber.

Fiona smiled.

Yes, that's it. That's her future.

Fiona could hardly contain her excitement. At any second her baby's first sweet words would mark the beginning of a journey towards realizing her vision. Her baby's voice would be the source of inspiration. It would captivate, be listened to and respected. It would bring peace and comfort.

Fiona sat her baby on her lap, filled with anticipation.

"Maaaammaaa," Fiona said, her eyes wide. "Say it, my angel... *Maaaammaaa."*

The baby's mouth opened wider and released a mighty belch. Serenity replaced the look of concentration on her round face.

Fiona sighed.

Gas, just gas.

Suddenly, her daughter peed. An incredible stream of urine flowed down Fiona's dress.

"Ewwwww!" Fiona cried as warm liquid gushed down her legs.

Fiona woke up with a jolt.

A book on pregnancy precariously balancing on her swollen belly fell to the floor.

Fiona had been feeling terribly ill all night, rushing to the bathroom hourly because of diarrhea and cramps. She suspected it was food poisoning. Now she had peed in her bed, an embarrassment she thought she had outgrown when she was 5-years old.

Shit, the bed is soaked.

Disoriented with sleep, Fiona heaved her enormous pregnant frame off the bed. She unsteadily wobbled to the bathroom and flicked on the light switch.

The haziness of sleep dissipated as Fiona stared at the clear fluid that continued to pour down her legs. It was not urine but amniotic fluid.

Fiona gasped as she was struck with a contraction. She bent forward from the pain.

Oh God, I'm in labor!

Fear and excitement seized her.

She called out for help.

*   *   *   *   *

"I'm here!" Ayden cried.

He ran into the bedroom and tripped over the red birth ball.

Fiona, eyes closed and laying on a chux-pad laden bed, moaned as she pressed hot compresses against her swollen abdomen, concentrating on her contraction.

Mrs. Flaherty, a 68-year old midwife, stuck her head out from between Fiona's legs, frowning at the disruption.

Hanna Walker, Fiona's widowed mother, rushed into the bedroom with a tray of wet towels.

"There you are, Ayden!" she said, as she stepped over him. "Get up and be useful."

Ayden stood up and caught the wet towel thrown at him.

Once the contraction passed, Fiona collapsed against the dozen pillows packed behind her. She opened her eyes and smiled at Ayden, who took her hand.

"I'm glad you're here," she said.

He gently wiped the sweat off her brow with the towel.

"How are you?"

"Back is hurting...tired...but she's just getting warmed up."

"Still think it's a girl, eh?" Ayden asked with a smile.

"I've seen her."

"What took you so long, anyway?" Hanna Walker demanded.

Ayden sighed.

"You know I was on a flight over the Atlantic, Hanna. I couldn't exactly turn the plane around, could I?"

"I've told you to call me 'Mama,'" she said coldly.

"As soon as I landed at Heathrow I took the first flight back, *Hanna*."

"Yer a pilot?" Mrs. Flaherty asked, her Scottish accent as sharp as her piercing look.

The midwife warily eyed his smartly pressed uniform.

"Co-pilot."

Mrs. Flaherty snorted, unimpressed. She disappeared again between Fiona's legs.

"We sent word to you that Fiona went into labor 12 hours ago!" Mama said, unwilling to drop the subject.

"That's how long it takes to cross the Atlantic and back," Ayden said, exasperated. "I'm sorry I was away. I should have been here."

"That's okay," Fiona said. "You're here now."

"No, it's not. You knew Fiona was close to term, Ayden. If you took any responsibility—"

"Mama, drop it," Fiona said softly.

"Have you eaten anything?" Ayden asked Fiona.

He was concerned at how tired and frail she looked. The dark circles around her sunken eyes accentuated her pasty, clammy skin.

How is she going to have the strength to do this? he worried.

"Echinacea, vitamin C, and red raspberry leaf tea. All day, pills and flavored water. No real food," Mama said, turning her anger towards her daughter.

Masking his concern, Ayden gently stroked her hair.

"Fiona, you have to eat something to keep your strength up," he said.

"She won't listen," Mama said. "Dr. Connie has brainwashed her."

"Not Dr. Connie, Fiona," Ayden groaned. "She's a television quack!"

"She's a brilliant doctor," Fiona replied, yawning.

"She received her doctorate from the Internet!"

"Yeah, I know, but–ah!"

"Another contraction?"

Fiona nodded.

"Ah, ah, ah..."

"That was fast," he breathed.

"Aye, they're about 2 minutes apart," Mrs. Flaherty said, completing her examination. "Fiona, you're 7 centimeters dilated. You're looking bonny, dear, but your cervix has a wee anterior lip. Nae' to worry about, though, I assure you. It should clear up when you're fully dilated."

"And the baby?" Mama asked.

"Based on the baby's heartbeat and Fiona's back pain, I think the baby may be posterior."

Ayden and Mama exchanged looks of concern.

"Tis a common thing, Mrs. Walker, it is. Usually the baby turns before descending the birth canal. No need for concern, I assure you."

"...hee, hee, hee..."

"Remember what I told you, Fiona, dear. Keep your voice low," the midwife said. "Oooooo."

"Oooooo," Fiona moaned.

She immediately felt a little better as the vibrations from her voice softened the pain.

Mrs. Flaherty nodded with approval.

"Aye, good, that's it, dear. Shan't be long now."

*   *   *   *   *

Fiona wept on her hands and knees as hot water from the shower splashed on her lower back.

She had tried every posture in search of a comfortable position as she labored. Only sitting on the birth ball had helped for some time, relaxing her pelvis and improving dilation, gravity assisting the delivery. But after a few hours the discomfort returned and the pain worsened. Unable to find any other comfortable position, Fiona had agreed to try the shower. Although the shower provided some relief for her back pain, the cramps from her contractions became increasingly intolerable.

The contraction ended, and Fiona instantly fell asleep, still on her hands and knees. After 24 hours of labor she was utterly exhausted. Sleeping between her contractions, however, made the pain feel continuous, never-ending, which intensified Fiona's despair.

Fiona's mother popped her head in the shower.

"Is the shower helping, honey?"

Fiona did not answer.

"Fiona!"

"Huh? What?"

The next powerful contraction struck Fiona. Her tailbone exploded with pain.

Wailing, she curled into a fetal position.

Mrs. Flaherty and Mama waited until the contraction passed before helping Fiona out of the shower. Ayden remained in the bedroom. The two women fit Fiona with a loose dress and carefully assisted her back into bed.

"*Oh God!*" Fiona cried as the next contraction struck.

"Yer 9 centimeters dilated, dear. The baby is almost ready to come," Mrs. Flaherty said after examining her.

"We must take her to the hospital," Mama said.

She brushed aside her tears. She couldn't bear to watch her daughter suffer any longer.

"No...no, hospital," Fiona gasped.

"Honey, we have to give you something to ease the pain. This is taking too much of a toll on you."

The contraction passed.

"No, Mama. Please, this is important to me," Fiona said, as she caught her breath. "I *must* have a natural birth. I want to feel her come out of me. I won't ruin this miracle by being numb and incoherent on drugs."

"But, Fiona, honey, you're in too much pain. How much more can you take? An epidural will ease your suffering. There is nothing wrong with it. I did it. All women do it."

"Not all women," Mrs. Flaherty muttered.

The midwife ignored the dark look from Mama.

"No epidural, Mama," Fiona said with conviction.

"Honey, you've been in labor for over 24 hours. You may need a C-section to get this baby out!"

Fiona affectionately rubbed her belly.

"She doesn't want to leave me," she said with a tired smile.

"But you may be in danger!"

"Oh, no, Mama. She'll never hurt me...my angel," Fiona whispered and then passed out.

"Fiona? Fiona!" Mama cried.

"You heard her, Mrs. Walker. She said, 'no,'" Mrs. Flaherty said. "Now, let her be."

Mama glared venomously at the midwife.

"Why do you encourage her? This natural birth may kill my daughter and grandchild."

"You underestimate your girl, Mrs. Walker. She's a fighter, she is. She and that baby of hers got a fire that will nae' be extinguished. She'll be fine, I assure you."

"With all due respect, Mrs. Flaherty, delivering a child is very different than having one. *I* know what Fiona is going through."

Mrs. Flaherty's face flushed with anger.

"Wi' all dae respect, Mrs. Walker, quit yer blatherin! I've had *8* children, all boys over 10 pounds, with nae' fancy hospitals or medicine. In my days back in Scotland, all I had was a piece of wood between me teeth to get through things. No one gave a *damn* how I felt, least of all my good-for-nothing drunkard husband—God bless his soul."

Mama was speechless. She desperately turned to Ayden, searching for an ally.

"What do you think, Ayden?"

Ayden sat by Fiona's side, and had listened silently. He took his time to speak, and when he did his voice was filled with authority.

"Mrs. Flaherty, is Fiona in any danger right now?"

"No. All of this is normal, I assure you. Thirty years of delivering babies tells me so."

"You call *this* normal?" Mama shouted.

"Aye, that I do," Mrs. Flaherty said confidently. "Fiona is near the end of her transition period and almost fully dilated. Won't be long now, that's a promise. May I add that I am responsible for Fiona and her baby, and we will go to the hospital if I deem it is necessary."

Ayden nodded.

"Very well, Mrs. Flaherty, I will trust your professional judgment."

"But—" Mama began.

Ayden raised his hand. Mama gaped with surprise.

"We should be supporting and comforting Fiona, Hanna, not questioning her choices or frightening her. Remember: Fiona has wanted a natural birth at home ever since she discovered she was pregnant. This is want she wants. There's nothing more to discuss."

Her face filled with rage, Mama stormed out of the bedroom. She slammed the door behind her.

"Mrs. Flaherty, if there's the slightest danger for Fiona or that baby, I expect you to tell me immediately. Are we clear?"

The midwife looked at the young man with newfound respect.

"Aye, sir, perfectly."

*　　　*　　　*　　　*　　　*

"Yer 10 centimeters, dear," Mrs. Flaherty said. "And the baby's turned, which is good news. But you still have a wee anterior lip. Now, this will hurt a wee bit, but I'll try to push the cervix away from the baby's heed."

Fiona's scream was terrifying as Mrs. Flaherty

tried to manipulate the cervix. After several moments, Fiona begged the midwife to stop.

"I must, dear, otherwise you could damage your cervix."

"I don't care! *Stop it!*"

Mrs. Flaherty reluctantly ceased the manipulations. She concealed her concern as she noticed Ayden closely scrutinizing her, and hoped the lip would vanish.

After a half dozen more contractions, Mrs. Flaherty was relieved to find the anterior lip gone.

Fiona could now feel the baby's head moving down her cervix. It felt as if the baby's skull was scraping against her cervix. The pain was excruciating, something none of the books she read had prepared her for.

Ayden stayed by Fiona's side. He somehow sensed when to comfort and sooth her with words, when to remain silent and squeeze her hand, put a cool cloth on her head, or massage her chapped lips with ice cubes. Although she was practically incoherent with pain, Fiona knew she wouldn't have been able to endure her agony if it had not been for his support. She was eternally grateful.

"Okay, dear, are you ready? It's time to push," Mrs. Flaherty said.

"Hurts..." Fiona said, in a foggy daze, half-asleep.

"I know, dear, but you have to push."

"...can't..."

"You want the pain to stop, don't you, dear?"

"...yes...epidural..."

"It's too late for that, dear."

"...no...no..."

"Fiona?"

"...tired..." she whispered, drifting.

"Fiona, dear?"

Fiona remained silent.

Mama and Ayden glanced at the midwife with concern.

Mrs. Flaherty examined the blood pressure and heart rate of the baby from a portable fetal scalp electrode that she inserted through the dilated cervix and attached to the baby's head. She then checked Fiona's heartbeat and blood pressure.

Her frown lessened. Both baby and mother were still doing well.

As the next contraction came Fiona shook her head and moaned.

"Please, no more..."

"Dear?"

"...make it stop..."

"Focus on my voice, dear."

"...sleep..."

Fiona closed her eyes again.

She was suddenly lying in the back seat of a car. Rain hammered the vehicle, distorting the world outside. A burly silhouette pressed his weight on top of her. His lips curled into a menacing smile, his eyes wild with lust.

"No!" she screamed. *"NO!"*

"Fiona, listen to me!" Mrs. Flaherty said sharply, shaking her. "Fiona!"

The midwife's sharp words punctured Fiona's dream. She opened her eyes and focused on the old woman.

"You okay, dear?"

Fiona nodded, tears filling her eyes.

"Good. Now, listen. If you want the pain to stop you have to get the baby out now. Understand?"

"Uh huh."

"Push if you want the pain to stop. Push, dear, *push!*"

Fiona grunted as she pushed with all her might. After the third push, Fiona threw up all over herself.

"I'm sorry!" she wept, ashamed.

"Ah, don't worry, dear. That was a good thing, I assure you. Throwing up is one of the best ways to push. It puts excellent pressure on the perineum."

Fiona felt better after her mother cleaned her up. Vomiting had disintegrated her sleepiness, and the urge to push was becoming overpowering.

Grinding her teeth, Fiona focused on her pushing.

"I can see the crown," Mrs. Flaherty said calmly. "Fiona, feel your baby's heed."

Fiona reached down and gasped as she fingered the soft, gooey flesh.

"I feel it!" she said, her eyes wide.

A surge of revitalized energy propelled her.

"Now, like we practiced, push. Push, dear. Push for the love of the Virgin Mary. *Push!*"

Discovering reserves of strength she didn't know she possessed, Fiona pushed with all her might.

"Ayden, grab Fiona's leg and hold her knee to her shoulder. Yes, that's it, lad, good. Mrs. Walker, take hold of Fiona's other leg and do the same."

Fiona screamed as she pushed again, oblivious to Ayden and Mama pressing her knees up to her shoulders.

"Relax and breathe, honey!" Mama said.

Unable to speak, Fiona glared at her mother. How the hell was she supposed to relax if she was pushing?

"Fiona, dear, breathe with me," Mrs. Flaherty said. "Two deep breaths and then hold as you push. Follow me, okay?"

Fiona nodded and followed her example.

It's working, Fiona thought with awe as the contraction passed. She had felt the baby slide back up after her push.

It was almost over!

"Okay, this should be it. One more, dear, I promise. You can do this. *Focus!*"

Fiona clutched the sheets, her fists white, and released a tormented scream that sent chills down Ayden's spine. It was as if she was being tortured.

"The heed is out," said the midwife. "I see the shoulders. Okay, Fiona, you can stop pushing."

Fiona continued to scream and push.

"Fiona, stop! You'll hurt yourself, dear!" Mrs. Flaherty said.

Fiona kept pushing, determined to get the baby out. She did not care what damage she caused herself.

Mrs. Flaherty sighed as the rest of the bloody, purplish baby slid out. No matter how many babies she had delivered, she always was washed with relief after a successful delivery.

Fiona exhaled with relief. The pain was gone.

She collapsed on the bed, spent. Her hair and dress were plastered to her body.

Mrs. Flaherty turned to Ayden. "Okay, time to cut the umbilical cord."

Ayden paled. "What? No, I can't."

"You made this request earlier, lad. Don't back out on me now."

The midwife handed him a surgical blade.

"Go on, Ayden," Fiona said with a tired smile. "I trust you."

"Wait until the umbilical cord stops pulsating," the midwife instructed.

As Mrs. Flaherty cradled the baby, Ayden held the umbilical cord and closed his eyes. He released a burst of air he didn't even know was trapped in his lungs as the blade sliced through the cord.

The midwife nodded with approval, and rubbed the baby.

A healthy wail escaped the newborn, a sound that brought Fiona tears of joy.

Mrs. Flaherty put the squirming infant in Fiona's arms. Fiona was surprised at how burning hot and slimy the tiny body felt.

"Well, what is it, sweetheart?" Mama exclaimed.

Fiona's crying intensified. "A girl. It's a beautiful girl."

"A job well done, lad," Mrs. Flaherty said to Ayden.

Ayden nodded, his face green, and bolted into the bathroom. The sound of him retching brought a smile to Fiona and Mama. The midwife scowled.

"Let me get her cleaned up, dear," Mrs. Flaherty said.

The midwife took the baby and examined her. After a few minutes the old woman proudly gave a APGARs rating of 10, and announced a weight at 8 pounds and 9 ounces, both signs of a perfectly healthy baby.

The baby stopped crying after Mrs. Flaherty bathed her and wrapped her tightly in a blanket. She handed the baby back to Fiona.

"You *are* an angel," Fiona said emotionally, cradling her baby.

Mother and child gazed at each other, deep brown eyes into large bluish-gray.

How can you be here and not inside me? Fiona wondered with amazement. *It's like you've always been here in my arms. You feel so right, so perfect—a miracle.*

A feeling of responsibility and absolute, boundless love settled upon Fiona. She never wanted this moment to end.

"You did it, honey. I'm so proud of you," Mama wept.

"I love you, Mama," Fiona cried, understanding for the first time how her mother truly felt about her.

As mother and grandmother embraced, Mrs. Flaherty focused her attention on the afterbirth.

The midwife frowned as Fiona pushed out the double-lobed placenta. The cord was attached to the placenta's side rather than its center. It was a potentially dangerous placenta and cord placement, and the old woman was relieved that the baby had delivered with minimal difficulty.

Ayden walked unsteadily back into the bedroom, groaning. His nausea returned at the sight of the misshapen placenta and the smell of warm blood. Covering his mouth, he ran back into the bathroom.

The midwife pulled out a medical sewing kit and mended a second-degree tear Fiona had suffered during the delivery. There was also severe bruising, and the midwife knew Fiona would be sore for several days.

"What do you think, Mrs. Flaherty?" Fiona asked, once the midwife finished stitching her.

"I've delivered many babies in my time, dear, and that perhaps is the most beautiful one I've seen, I assure you," she said, her eyes dancing, a hint of a smile gracing her lips.

"Do you want me to take the baby while you rest, Fiona?" Mama asked.

Fiona did not respond. She snored peacefully, her sleeping infant held protectively against her bosom.

*   *   *   *   *

Fiona glanced through the back window of the car. Rivulets of water streamed down the glass and blurred the rain-splattered scene. She found the drumming raindrops against the roof of the car unnerving.

"Well?" he asked gently, putting his muscular arm around her.

"I-I don't know," Fiona said.

"What don't you know?"

"I'm scared."

"Of what?"

"I don't know."

"You trust me, right?"

"Yes, you know I do."

"And we love each other, right?"

"Always," she whispered, losing herself in his liquid, confident eyes.

"Then?"

He smiled as he stroked her hair.

They kissed passionately.

Fiona tensed as his hand moved from her breast down towards her skirt.

"No...wait..."

"It'll be okay, babe," he said.

He reached for her panties.

"No, please..."

"It'll feel good, I promise," he said hoarsely.

He moved on top of her.

"No, stop...I don't want to..."

Fiona feebly tried to struggle as he roughly, frantically tore her panties.

He was too strong.

"*Stop!*"

He pinned her arms and smiled.

"STOP!"

Fiona awoke with a start.

Her heart pounded in her chest, the pain between her legs dull and throbbing.

She was in her room. It was dark outside. Ayden slept in the chair beside her bed. The baby was still asleep, her little head resting comfortably against the warmth of Fiona's breast.

Fiona forgot her disturbing dream as she gazed at her daughter. She could not believe how this tiny, delicate life was safe in her arms, so beautiful and innocent. For so many months they had been a part of each other—connected. Now, they were apart, two individuals, each with their own path and destiny.

Tears welled in Fiona's eyes.

Giving birth had taught her a heartbreaking lesson of motherhood: with love came necessary separations. It was a painful fact, and one Fiona would never forget.

"Whatever has happened or will happen, you are worth it," Fiona said softly to her daughter. "You will always be worth it...God, I love you so much. Why do I love you so much? My love for you hurts more than a thousand deliveries. Why does it have to hurt so bad?"

Ayden opened his eyes, and smiled at Fiona.

"Hey, there."

Fiona did not reply, brushing away her tears.

"You okay?" he asked.

"Uh huh."

Ayden's eyes fell onto the baby. He shook his head with bewilderment.

"I can't believe how small she is. Look at her little fingers. They look so delicate. I can't explain it, but I want to protect her from everything, you know?"

Fiona was filled with peace and love from Ayden's words. She knew exactly what Ayden felt, and held her baby closer against her.

"You'll make a wonderful uncle, Ayden."

"I doubt it, sis. I've already bought the shotgun for when she starts dating," Ayden chuckled. "Hey, Fiona, you did great. Really. I can't believe my little sister is a moth—"

Ayden caught himself and sighed.

"She certainly gave you a difficult delivery, didn't she?"

Fiona smiled sadly. "She didn't want to leave me."

Mama quietly entered the room. She sat by the edge of the bed and watched her daughter interact with her granddaughter. Fiona ignored her. Mama opened her mouth, but was unable to muster the words. She looked desperately at her son for help.

Ayden turned to his sister.

"Fiona, Claire and Steven Dawson are downstairs. They've been waiting."

Mama nodded as her daughter looked at her, searching for guidance. Mama struggled to control the remorse and conflict on her face. No matter how difficult, she had to be strong for both of them.

Fiona bit her lip. Her eyes focused back on her baby.

"Fiona, honey?"

"She must be hungry. I should feed her," Fiona said.

"Mrs. Flaherty fed her while you were asleep," Mama said softly.

Tears fell on her newborn's face.

"Fiona?" Mama said softly.

She did not respond.

"Honey, it's...it's for the best."

"Send them in," Fiona whispered.

"I'll get them," Ayden said, and left the room.

The Dawsons entered the bedroom. Holding hands, they approached the bed.

Fiona kissed her newborn on the forehead. She prayed for forgiveness.

Claire Dawson stepped forward.

"Hey, Fiona," she said softly, afraid that Fiona might change her mind. "How are you feeling?"

Fiona looked at the woman who had yearned to have a baby her entire life.

Fiona had interviewed the Dawsons six months earlier. The couple's prominent professions, devotion for each other, and love for children had convinced Fiona that she had made the right choice for her baby.

Fiona held up the baby. The wrenching pain in her watery eyes betrayed her brave expression.

"Claire, meet Angel, your new daughter," said the 15-year old.

Glossary

As-salaam-alaikum: Islamic greeting meaning: "Peace be with you."

APGAR: a scoring system devised to measure the healthiness of a newborn (A = activity and muscle tone; P = pulse; G = grimace and reflex irritability; A = appearance and skin color; R = respiration).

areé: "hey" in Hindi.

autorickshaw: a motorized version of traditional rickshaws. The autorickshaw is characterized by a tin or iron body resting on three wheels (two wheels in the rear and one in the front). It is generally black and yellow in color, has no doors, and has a canopy on top. Instead of a steering wheel, autorickshaw's are steered with a handlebar for control, effectively making them a three-wheeler motorcycle with passengers in the rear.

beta: "son," "daughter," or "my child," in Hindi.

bhai: "brother" in Hindi.

bidi: leaf-wrapped tobacco.

birth ball: a large, sturdy ball that women sit on for comfort during labor. A birth ball allows expecting women to simultaneously rest their legs while still requiring them to move their pelvis to help the baby find the best position to travel down the birth canal.

blatherin: Scottish slang, which means: "to talk nonsense."

Blimey: British slang, meaning: "bloody hell."

Blyat: Russian profanity, meaning : "fuck."

bonny: "healthy," or "pretty" or "beautiful" in Scottish.

chapatti: flat, round piece of bread

chhee: "yuck" or "gross."

chottu: "little one."

chux-pad: A large, flat disposable pad consisting

of thick layers of highly absorbent material and a waterproof backing.

crore: "ten-million" in Hindi.

daal: "lentils" in Hindi.

dae: "due" in Scottish.

dhoti: a long, cotton loincloth worn by Hindu men.

duffer: "fool" or "moron" in Hindi.

Hain-nah?: "right?" in Hindi.

heed: "head" in Scottish.

kurta pajama: a loose, comfortable shirt without a collar that extends to the knees and matching loose pants. Generally worn by men on the Indian subcontinent.

Mahatma: Great Soul

namasté: "hello" or "goodbye" in Hindi.

nah?: "eh?" in Hindi.

nae': "no" or "not" in Scottish

rupees: Indian currency.

sahib: "sir" in Hindi.

samosa: a deep-fried pastry filled with vegetables or meat.

sari: an outer garment generally worn by women on the Indian subcontinent. A sari consists of a length of cloth made from cotton or silk, with one end wrapped about the waist to form a skirt, and the other end draped over the shoulder or covering the head.

Sri: "Mr." in Hindi

Wa-alaikum-as-salaam: Islamic response to being greeted, meaning: "And may peace be with you."

wallah: a person who specializes in that trade

wee: meaning "little," "slight," or "young" in Scottish.

_wi':_ "with" in Scottish.

yer: "you're" or "your" in Scottish.

About The Author

Shaun spent a year in India living the experiences that are captured in his first novel, *Divya's Dharma*. The novel depicts the physical and spiritual journey of Divya—a young Indian woman born and raised in Canada—who travels to Southern India for the first time as an exchange student. There, she is overwhelmed by the country's beauty and hypocrisy. When Divya confronts her family's past and the horrors of caste oppression, a series of events are triggered that shape and change her life forever.

A Slice of Life is Shaun's second book. The first short story in the book, *Amal,* has been adapted to a short film by Richie Mehta. *Amal* was filmed on the streets of New Delhi to capture the integrity of the story. It was shown at the 2004 Montreal World Festival, the 2004 Palm Springs International Festival of Short Films, and the 2004 Telluride Film Festival. *Amal* won Best Short Film in Canada at the 2005 Reel World Film Festival. To learn more about this film, please go to: ***www.poormansproductions.com.***

Shaun is completing his third novel, *Deceptive Shadows,* which is part a Medieval Fantasy and part a contemporary Suspense Thriller. He is also currently working on a feature-length screenplay for *Amal.*

Shaun has an International MBA, an Honors Bachelors of Business Administration, and a Bachelors of Education. He lives and teaches in Toronto.

To learn more about Shaun and his work, please go to: ***www.shaunmehta.com.***

Printed in the United States
34487LVS00001B/157-315